Sleep Little One

Hitman

USA TODAY BESTSELLING AUTHORS
C. HALLMAN
ISABELLA STARLING

Copyright © 2021 by C. Hallman

Cover Design by C. Hallman

Bleeding Heart Covers

All rights reserved.

No part of this book may be reproduced in any form or by any electronic or mechanical means, including information storage and retrieval systems, without written permission from the author, except for the use of brief quotations in a book review.

1

ALARIC

"Please, man. I'm fucking begging you. All I need is a few more days. Can't you just tell your boss that?"

"You had days." I cock the gun I have aimed at him. "You had weeks. Months. It's over."

"Don't do this." The man runs his fingers through his graying hair, and I watch him impassively. All I have left to do is pull the trigger because nothing he says will change my mind. "Please, man, fuck! Don't fucking shoot or—"

I don't let him finish his sentence. I fire the gun and watch the bullet bury itself between his eyes. Blood spurts from what used to be his head and soils the dark alleyway. I'm not cleaning up this mess. This is a shitty part of town, so no one's going to give a damn anyway.

Kneeling next to the body, I take his wallet and phone. No one will suspect foul play because I've made it look like a robbery.

I throw one last look at what's left of Daniel Newman. He's had this coming for a long fucking time now. The person who ordered this hit has been trying to get his money back for years. Nobody will miss Daniel, either. Being single with no kids, he's left no mark on this sick, twisted world.

I pocket the wallet and phone and head around the back alley with my gun tucked in the back of my pants. This particular alley does not contain security cameras, which makes it the perfect place for a hit. I've never been here before, but my curiosity is piqued as I round the corner and watch a group of barely legal girls in bondage gear enter the club.

It's been a few days since I got my cock sucked, and I'm itching for a willing victim to bury myself in. Maybe I can stick around for a while longer and see what Purgatory has to offer. Judging by the bait outside, I'll find exactly what I'm looking for.

Ignoring the long queue in front of the club, I cut to the front and smirk at one of the thugs guarding the entrance.

"Where the fuck do you think you're going?" he snarls at me. But all it takes to change his scornful look is one flash of the red ribbon tied around my wrist. He knows what it means. I work for the Lombardi family.

Clearing his throat, the goon steps aside and allows me to pass. I walk inside the darkness, parting the red velvet curtains to enter Purgatory.

The excitement in this place is fucking palpable. Girls are dancing in cages, and people mill about, eyeing each other. At least a dozen people wait in front of the bar to get an order in. Ignoring all of them, I push my way into their midst, my eyes searching for someone who knows how to mix a halfway decent drink.

When I see her for the first time, my reaction is instantaneous. My cock jumps to attention like it wants to fucking salute her. Straining against the fabric of my black pants, I can feel the precum leaking out of my tip like a goddamn faucet.

Her honey-blond hair falls off her shoulders in loose waves, and I have the urge to run my fingers through her locks so I can figure out if it feels as soft as it looks.

"An old-fashioned," I request loud and clear. The sexy little vixen working the bar raises her baby blue eyes to mine, and I do nothing to hide the fact I'm fucking devouring her with my gaze.

"Coming right up," she says, giving me a nod. I watch her mix the drink. She knows what she's doing, and my cock grows more, straining against my pants painfully. She presents me with the drink and holds out her hand for my credit card. Smirking, I hand her my black Amex and watch her swipe it without reacting. When she hands it back, I wrap my hand around her wrist, holding her in place. Even over the music playing, I can hear her sharp intake of breath.

"Take a break," I mutter, loud enough for just us to hear. "Meet me out back in five. I'm going for a cigarette."

"I..." Her eyes bore into mine. I don't wait for her answer before taking my glass and walking outside into the smokers' area. Standing beside the two guys making out and the one lone wolf thoughtfully smoking a cigarette, I pull out my own pack and light the stick of poison, inhaling the smoke.

That's the fucking shit. Nothing feels as good as the first inhale after a goddamn kill.

"You wanted to see me?"

I lift my eyes slowly, lazily, until they meet the waitress's from the bar. I give myself ample time, allowing my gaze to drink her in. Every curve, every strand of light hair is instantly committed to memory. She's fucking sex on legs with a tight little waist, big tits, and an ass I want to palm over the fabric of her little black excuse for a dress.

"Why'd you come?" I ask, putting out my cigarette. She takes a step closer, drinking me in. She seems observant enough. Yet it fucking amuses me to no end that she hasn't noticed she's talking to a fucking monster.

"I was due for a break," she says. "Thought I'd get some fresh air."

"In the smokers' lounge?" I smirk. "Sure, sugar."

She blinks rapidly at the nickname, and a smile tugs on the corners of her lips. "Maybe I'm a smoker too."

"You're not." I laugh.

"How do you know?"

"You seem too smart to be a smoker," I mutter, pulling back from the wall. "You want to make some money?"

"Money?" Her brows knit together.

"I have five grand if you want it."

"For what?"

"What do you think?" I smirk. "I want my cock sucked. I don't pay for pussy, but I will pay for you to wrap that pretty little mouth around my cock and suck it dry."

"I'm not a whore," she spits out, turning around to leave just as the couple walks out. I grab her by the wrist and pull her back to me, and she doesn't even fucking fight it. I glare at the lone straggler left in the lounge until he rolls his eyes and leaves as well. Now it's just us. No fucking witnesses.

I could do whatever the fuck I wanted to her now. My employers would cover my tracks, and nobody would know.

I may be a hitman, but I'm not a fucking monster. When she puts her mouth on my dick, it'll be consensual. In fact, I won't shoot my load down her throat until she's begged for it.

"You don't do this for money?" I mutter against the shell of her ear. I can see goose bumps erupting all over her skin.

"No," she hisses.

"So you'll do it for free?"

She yanks her arm out of my hold and glares at me. "I'm not going to suck your dick. Not for any amount of money."

She's cute when she lies. She has a tell, too. She blinks fast, once, twice. I already know her biggest secret.

"What's your name?"

She looks like she won't answer, but then she changes her mind and mutters, "Monroe."

"How old are you, Monroe?"

Her eyes fill with panic. "What does it matter?"

"You twenty-one?" She doesn't answer, just stares at me. "You shouldn't be serving drinks."

"I do whatever I have to," she mutters.

"So you do need the money."

She doesn't reply. Her mouth thins into a line, and she glares at me. "Not that badly."

"Really?" I smirk. "Everyone has a price, Monroe. What's yours?"

"You can't buy me."

"I can't? Not even a kiss?"

"I..." She looks away. I can tell she's struggling with her decision. I'm fucking loving this. "I don't know."

"Here." I pull out my wallet. It's thick with hundred-dollar bills. I peel off some and hand them to her. "Two grand. For a kiss."

Her eyes widen at the sight of the money. "I can't take this."

I grab her by the waist. Her eyes widen with a mix of fear and lust as I pull her against me. I don't wait for her to argue; I just fucking kiss her. Her lips are sweet and taste like bubblegum. She doesn't fight me. She even parts her lips for me, allowing my tongue to meet hers and fucking take whatever the hell I want.

When I pull back, her face is flushed, and she looks crestfallen.

"Here," I say, handing her the bills. "I owe you now."

She eyes the money. Monroe seems hungry for it, but I can tell her pride prevents her from taking it. I tuck the bills into her bra without touching her skin, just the fabric of her lingerie peeking out from under her dress. My cock tightens again.

"Thank you, sugar." I smirk, walking away from her.

Just as I'm about to enter the club again, she calls out for me, saying, "Wait!"

I turn over my shoulder as she catches up with me, eyes wide. She hesitates, but I can tell there's a question on the tip of her tongue.

"Just say it." I grin.

"Do you... do you have more?" Fearfully, she raises her sweet eyes to mine.

"You saw my wallet, didn't you?" She nods, swallowing. "How much more do you need?"

She stares into my eyes, her bottom lip trembling as she whispers, "A-All of it. P-Please."

I want to laugh out loud, but at the same time, I'm consumed with fucking guilt. This shit doesn't happen to me. I don't have a moral code, yet this girl is making me question my actions just by batting her lashes at me.

"What are you going to do for it?"

"I..." She bites her bottom lip, perfect pearly whites digging into her juicy little mouth. "Whatever you want."

I shouldn't go along with this. She's not even fucking twenty-one. She doesn't deserve for me to destroy her life, yet I can't stop myself. I want her. And she'll be rewarded, after all. It's not like I'm taking advantage.

"You got private rooms here?" I grunt.

"Yeah," she whispers.

"Let's go."

She walks ahead of me with purpose. But I don't miss the tremble of her hands when she retrieves a key card from behind the counter. I don't miss the way her eyes keep darting around the room. I don't miss *any*-fucking-thing.

Unlike her, I'm calm as fucking ever. I follow her upstairs down a long hallway with several doors. She opens one of them and steps inside, and I follow her in. The room's a pretty basic BDSM dungeon with a huge heart-shaped bed and various implements and equipment peppered around the place. I can already think of a few *very* fucking fun things to do to Monroe in here.

"W-What do you want to do?" she stutters, flushing.

"I want you to make me another drink." I shrug off my jacket and place it on the bed. "Turn on some music. I'm going to watch you."

She nods, eyes avoiding mine as she puts on some sensual music through the speakers. She starts mixing a drink at the bar in the corner of the room, but she's so nervous a glass slips from her hand and shatters on the floor.

"Fuck," she whispers, leaning down to pick it up.

"Leave it."

"No, but I—"

"Leave it."

She obeys, and it pleases me. My cock is as hard as a goddamn rock right now, picturing her doing more for me, submitting to me. I wonder how fucking often she does this. How many times has she let a stranger pay for a kiss, a blow job, a fuck? I don't give a shit about any of the others before me. Tonight, Monroe is my property.

I hand her another glass. "Drink, please."

She takes a deep breath and mixes another old-fashioned. She hands me the drink, and our fingers brush as I take it from her. I sit down on a leather armchair and watch her nervously fidgeting with the hem of her tight little dress.

"Don't you want to...?" She flushes at the sound of her own words. "You know..."

I shake my head. "Not yet. First, you're going to do something for me."

Taking out my wallet, I place it on my knee. It's bulging from the number of bills inside, and Monroe eyes it hungrily.

"What do you want me to do?" she asks in a soft whisper.

"I want you to dance," I say firmly. "I want you to look me right in the eyes, strip off your clothes, and dance for me. If you're a good girl, I'll give you more money. And other things, too. But you'll have to ask for it."

Her eyes flash with anger. "You want me to beg for money?"

"No, sugar." I smirk. "I want you to beg for my cock."

2
MONROE

I've lost count of the number of times Lucian has asked me to work upstairs, to sell my body so someone could live out their fantasies. I've told him no, time and time again, insisting I'd never be that desperate.

Oh, how the mighty have fallen.

I've never condemned the other girls from doing it, never thought less of them, but not in a million years did I think I'd be here.

"Don't let me wait, Monroe." He says my name as though he owns it, then leans back into the chair as if it were custom-made for him. He exudes confidence in everything he does and every word he speaks. A confidence that I envy and admire deeply, especially right now as I am desperately trying to find my own.

Swallowing down my anxiety, I let my fingertip dance over the hem of my dress and start swaying my hips gently to the rhythm of the music.

While I do my little dance, I take a moment to check him out. He is tall with a handsome, rugged kind of face. From what I can tell with his clothes on, he stays in shape. He looks to be in his late thirties, maybe early forties judging by the few strands of gray hair. The rest of it is black, just like the clothes he is wearing.

The sleeves of his expensive-looking shirt are rolled up, black ink tattoos wrap around both of his forearms, making a single red ribbon on his wrist stand out. I've seen a few people with the red ribbon before, but I could never figure out what it means.

His eyes never leave mine as I let my hands glide up my body, tracing the outside of my breasts. Hooking my fingers under the thin straps, I slowly slide them down my shoulders one by one. Then I push them down my arms until they're hanging by my side without a purpose.

Reaching back, I fumble with the zipper of my dress, only then realizing how my hands are shaking. I keep a sensual smile plastered on my face, not giving away how nervous I actually am.

When I finally get the zipper pulled down, I shimmy out of the tight dress and let it fall to the floor. Gulping down the lump that formed in my throat, I stand before this stranger in nothing but my bra, thong, and high heels.

He rakes his gaze up and down my body slowly, almost like he is mapping every square inch of me. Even in the dim light and with his eyes hooded, I don't miss how his pupils are dilated and his hands twitch with anticipation.

Reaching back once more, I unclasp my bra. My boobs spill out, and I can't help but gasp at the way they feel heavier than usual. My nipples are tight, and there is an odd tingling sensation.

"Keep moving," he orders, making me realize I had stopped in the first place.

I continue rolling my hips, hyper aware of how my unrestrained tits sway with every small move I make.

My mouth goes dry, and a knot forms in the depth of my stomach as I lower my eyes briefly and catch sight of the massive bulge in his slacks.

A low chuckle fills the space, and I drag my eyes back up to his. Amusement flickers in his dark gaze, but is quickly lost in the sea of desire... desire for me.

Working at Purgatory meant I quickly got used to men ogling me with lustful eyes. But nothing has ever felt like this. Something is different about this guy. A darkness surrounds him like a thick cloak hiding him in the shadows.

He is an enigma, and something about that mystery has me intrigued. Maybe that's why I decided to take him up on his offer when I've turned so many down. That or the fact that I really need that money more than ever.

"I'm losing patience. Get rid of your panties, and let me see that pussy you're hiding."

Taking a deep breath, I dip my fingers into the waistband and push down the thin material. Cool air washes over my shaved pussy while my face feels like it has turned fifty shades of red.

My thong joins my dress and bra on the floor, leaving me standing in front of this stranger completely bare. No guy has ever seen me naked before. No one except him—a man I don't know.

I fight the urges to cover up while forcing myself to keep dancing. Uncertainty worms its way through my body. This was a mistake. I have no idea what I am doing here since I've never done anything like it.

I'm about to tell him the truth, but the thought of not getting the money has me pressing my lips together tightly.

"Remember what I want you to do next?" he suddenly asks.

I nod, chewing on my bottom lip nervously before opening my mouth. "I want you…" I start with good intentions but choke on the last few words.

"Go on, beg for my cock. Say the words, sugar."

"I want your… cock."

"I like how you play innocent"—he smirks—"as if you never had a cock in your mouth before."

God, he has no idea how much I'm not *playing.*

"Where do you want my cock?"

I swallow, and my tongue gets stuck to the roof of my mouth because there is no saliva left. It's so fucking dry, I can barely speak.

"I don't know. Wherever you want to put it."

With a loud groan, he tips his head back. "Fuck, my dick is so hard for you. Why don't you get on your knees and get it out so you can see for yourself."

Careful so as not to trip over my own two feet, I step out of the pile of discarded clothes and move between his legs. Lowering myself to the floor, I get on my knees in front of him.

Hesitantly, I reach for the zipper on his pants. Unable to avoid it, my fingers brush against his bulge, drawing another pained groan from his chest.

I pull the zipper down and undo the button. All that remains between me and his cock is the black fabric of his boxers. Dipping my finger into the waistband, I pull his boxers down, and his cock springs free.

It's even bigger than I thought. Thick veins are corded around the shaft, the mushroom-looking head is an angry purple color, and there is a shiny wet spot at the very tip.

"I want your sweet lips wrapped around it." His low and gravelly voice vibrates through my whole body.

Placing one hand on his knee, I lift my other one to his lap. He hisses when I wrap my fingers around the base of his shaft and lean in. I shift my weight, trying to scoot closer. The unforgiving cold concrete under my knees is a stark contrast to the warm and smooth skin of the dick in my hand.

"Open up, sugar."

I do as he says and open my mouth. Sticking out my tongue, I press it to the underside of his cock and close my lips around the tip. He tastes like he smells... musky, like the earth, untamed and wild.

"Fucking Christ, you're killing me," he groans and places both hands on each side of my face. His large, calloused palms rub against my skin as he drags his thumbs across my cheekbones gently.

Before I can even think about objecting, he pulls my head toward him, filling my mouth with enough of his huge cock to cause my gag reflex to kick in.

Instinctively, I try to pull away. Placing my hands on his knees, I shove at him, but he only tightens his grip on me.

"No backing out now. I'm too far gone to let you stop. You're going to suck this cock until I come down your pretty little throat."

Panic slithers up my spine as he takes control of my head, using my mouth for his pleasure. He starts out with shallow thrusts but quickly speeds up and goes deeper with every push. I gag around his length, but that only seems to egg him on further. Blinking away the tears, I watch his face closely as it twists in pleasure. He obviously enjoys this display of power because he's reveling in the way he has full control of me.

During his relentless assault, saliva starts running down my chin, and tears fall from the corners of my eyes. His thrusts become violent, and each one ends with the tip of his cock bumping against the back of my throat. My vision becomes blurry from both the tears and the lack of air. I let my eyes flutter shut.

"Yes," he grunts. "Close your eyes and keep them closed."

I follow his command. Squeezing my eyes shut, I concentrate on keeping my throat lax.

"I bet your cunt is nice and wet by now, wishing I would shove my cock in your tight hole." At his words, I squeeze my legs together. I want to shake my head but realize shamefully that there is in fact moisture between my folds.

"I'm sorry to disappoint your pussy, but I don't fuck girls like you."

I flinch at his words, which deem it a reminder of what exactly we are doing here. I'm offering my body for him to use me as he pleases. That's all this is and all it will ever be.

Relaxing my throat as much as I can, I let him do just that... use me.

After a few more brutal thrusts, he stills. His cock swells impossibly large, and a warm substance spills into the back of my throat. He holds me there for another moment, cutting off my air supply and making my head swim from the lack of oxygen.

When he finally lets go of me, I suck in air like I desperately need it. As I catch my breath, I watch his face in wonder, mesmerized by the display of absolute bliss. His head is tipped back, his eyes are closed, and his face is relaxed, making him look a few years younger. Something tells me he doesn't let himself experience this kind of pleasure often.

An odd sense of pride fills me. I made that happen. I made him feel like this.

That misplaced pride is quickly forgotten when he opens his eyes, and the haze of post-orgasm elation slips from his expression.

"That was really fucking good, but it's time for me to leave," he explains and starts tucking his half-hard cock back into his pants.

The salty taste he left behind on my tongue turns bitter at the realization of what I've just done. No matter how much I need this money, and no matter the reason, I still became a prostitute tonight.

Lost in thought, I flinch when he reaches out for me. Grabbing me under my arms, he lifts me up like an adult would a child. My legs are stiff as he comes to a stand and makes me stand in front of him. I'm still completely naked while he is completely clothed.

"Here." He shoves something at me, and when I lower my eyes, I realize it's a stack of one-hundred-dollar bills. "Take it," he urges.

My hand moves on its own, and I grab the wad of cash without a word.

"I'll see you around." And with that, he turns and leaves. I don't watch him walk out, but I hear the door open and shut. The air shifts with the absence of his body. The room suddenly feels larger, emptier, and colder. The only sounds that remain are the soft music in the background and the heavy beating of my heart.

I stand there for another moment, wearing nothing but a pair of heels with who knows how many thousands of dollars in my hand. Shame threatens to swallow me whole, and I know if I don't move soon, I will be here all night.

Shaking my head, I snap out of it. Putting the cash on the side table next to his half-finished drink, I gather my clothes from the floor and dress in a hurry. I quickly count the cash, which adds up to be eight thousand dollars.

Who carries that kind of cash on them?

A guy who came to a club to buy sex. The question is, why did he give me so much and ask for so little in return? Dumbfounded, I look around the room that holds a large selection of sex toys and furniture.

All thoughts leave my mind momentarily when I catch my reflection in the mirror over the bar. Black mascara streaks down my cheek, my hair is unruly, and my dress is rumpled. I look like the way I feel. *Used.*

Using some napkins and water, I remove the smeared mascara as best as I can before running my fingers through my hair like a comb. Only when I look somewhat presentable do I dare to leave the room and make my way downstairs. I somehow hold on to the belief that no one will know what I just did. But as I step into the staircase, Toni and Bruno—two of our bouncers— both look at me with an unmistakable comprehension in their eyes.

Making my legs move faster, I hurry down the stairs just to come to a sudden halt when Lucian steps into my way.

"Were you with a guy up there?" He points at the top of the stairs like he doesn't already know the answer.

"You don't have to rub it in my face, okay? You were right. I fucking did it."

"I don't give a shit about that, Monroe. Were you with a guy who had a red ribbon tied around his wrist?"

"Um, yeah."

"Shit, did he hurt you?" I'm surprised by the genuine concern in his voice.

"No, why?"

Lucian looks around, making sure no one is listening to our conversation. "He killed someone in the side alley before going up with you."

All air wooshes from my lungs. My head spins, and my stomach churns as I try to process Lucian's words.

"You must be mistaken. It's not true."

"Monroe, the red ribbon means he works for the Lombardis. Do you know who they are?" He pauses, probably waiting for me to answer, but when I don't, he continues. "They are bad news. They are the mob, Monroe. You can be glad you made it out of that room unharmed."

The stack of money in my bra suddenly feels like a thousand-pound weight. Fuck, what did I do? I let a guy pay me for a blow job.

A guy who works for the mob. A killer. I almost gave my virginity to him.

And I don't even know his fucking name.

3

ALARIC

I don't get hung up on pussy.

It's one of my rules and a way for me to keep my head clear. I fuck women once, and that's fucking it. Relationships are for the weak. My dick, however, is not.

Yet a few days later, I find myself unable to think about anything but the blue eyed vixen who sucked my cock so clumsily it felt like it was her first time. If I didn't know any better, I'd be convinced she was new at this shit. But the fact that she was so eager to take my money makes me think otherwise. She needed that cash.

Over the past few days, curiosity has started blooming in my mind. I'm wondering what she's going to spend the money on. Probably expensive bags, clothes, whatever the fuck girls like her buy. I do my best to push Monroe out of my head and away from my mind. Yet my thoughts keep circling back to her, imagining her life and wondering what she does when she isn't mixing drinks at Purgatory.

I fight it. I do everything I can to get her out of my head, but Monroe holds on for dear life. Four days after our fucked-up little encounter, I've finally had enough. I'm going to give in. I'm going to find her and make sure she's not being a dumb little bitch with the money I gave her.

Finding her is easy enough. With just a couple of calls, I have her address.

I've made a business of staying in the shadows. My nondescript sedan means I remain unnoticed as I turn onto her street, and I don't draw any extra attention from passersby. It's dark outside, dark and cool as the evening turns into night.

Monroe lives in a tiny house, one in a row of many on her street. She must share it with someone else, another girl who seems to be better off than Monroe. My little victim lives in the basement with a separate entrance. Her apartment looks fucking tiny. I'm guessing she makes a decent earning at Purgatory and could afford rent at a better place, so why the fuck is she living in this shit hole?

The girl is intriguing. My curiosity has piqued yet again, and I watch her come back home from a shift at Purgatory after midnight. She takes the basement entrance and lights a single bulb in her apartment. I watch her strip from her signature black dress and put on an oversized shirt to sleep in. My hands form fists, and I mutter a curse word under my breath. The girl isn't careful enough. She doesn't even shut the curtains to prevent some fucking creep from watching her change.

She's innocent.

So fucking different than me. I've been living in the darkness for as long as I can fucking remember. But not her, not Monroe. She's a creature that thrives in the light.

I told myself before I got here that I'd lose interest in her. But the opposite is happening now. I'm becoming more and more intrigued by Monroe, and it fucking pisses me off. I bury my nails into the skin of my palm, gritting my teeth. I don't have time for this shit.

And there's something else. Something that's calling me forward, telling me to leave my car and break into her shabby apartment. I want to watch her. I want to examine her.

Monroe is like a kill. I prepare for that the same way. By studying my victim's habits. Except I have no intention of hurting Monroe. Not unless she fucking begs for it.

Even though I know it's a bad idea, I get out of my car. I can't stay the fuck away. Something's pulling me to her, like an invisible string drawing me closer, nearer.

I take the stairs leading down to the basement entrance. There's still a light on inside even though there hasn't been any movement in a while. I grin at the thought. Seems like sugar's afraid of the dark because she leaves a light on at nighttime. Poor naïve little girl. If only she knew real monsters don't need the darkness to ruin her life...

I watch the window to make sure there's no movement, no sound. Once I'm sure she's asleep, I try the front door.

Locked.

But it's not as if that's going to keep me out.

Examining the small entrance, I take notice of a few empty flowerpots. It takes me less than a minute to find the spare key under one of them, and my lips press together into a painful line. Monroe doesn't know the first thing about taking care of herself, and it pisses me the fuck off.

Unlocking the front door, I place the key back where I found it and enter her apartment.

It's small. She's done her best to make the place look better, but there are things even Monroe can't fix, no matter how determined she is. Why the fuck does she live in this cramped and dingy place? Why the fuck doesn't she rent a nicer apartment?

Determined to get to the bottom of this, I start going through her things. Her bedroom door is closed at the end of the hallway. The temptation to go in there is strong, but I'm still resisting it. I'm saving the best for last.

The rest of the tiny apartment is even worse. A shitty, small bathroom with a rusty bathtub. A larger space for a minuscule kitchen with a single barstool at the counter. There's a laptop on the counter. No couch, no TV.

I approach the bedroom door. It's closed, but when I try the handle, I find it unlocked. I'm really fucking pushing it right now. If she wakes up, I'm going to have to hurt her. Yet I can't resist. I can't walk away. I need to see her again.

My fingers wrap around the cold doorknob. I twist it. Push it open.

Her bedroom's taken up by a small bed and a dresser. Light from the streetlight illuminates the small room through the window. Monroe's lying on the bed, covered with a thin, threadbare blanket. She's wearing that oversized shirt she put on earlier and no fucking panties. I can tell because her ass is peeking out. Firm, pale globes of skin draw my gaze and make me grit my fucking teeth.

Monroe's more complicated than I first gave her credit for. This apartment speaks of a story, something she's hiding, something she's doing. And I'm going to figure out what the fuck it is.

I stand frozen to the spot as she stirs in her sleep, but she doesn't wake up. She just lies on her back, her legs spread to give me a view of her perfect, shaved little pussy.

My mouth waters just as my phone goes off.

"Fuck," I hiss, checking to make sure she's still sleeping. She doesn't move. Her eyes flutter, but her breathing remains slow. She's asleep.

I'm resisting every urge in my body to touch her. My fingers itch to push up her shirt and touch her bare skin, but I fight the instinct. Instead, I palm the bulge in my pants, rubbing my hardened cock through the fabric of my black slacks.

Her lips are slightly parted. She looks so innocent like this. Ripe for the taking. But Monroe is hiding things. I know that already, and I'm determined to uncover what it is.

The inescapable lust forces me to pull down the zipper of my pants. I massage the bulge through the silky fabric of my boxers. I want so much more.

With a hiss, I pull out my cock, tapping my fingers on the soaked tip. I'm leaking already. I want nothing more than to wake up Monroe and have her suck the seed right out of my goddamn dick. But I fight the urge to do it. I have to.

I have no business getting involved with someone, least of all a little whore like Monroe. The memory of giving her that money is too fresh. To her, I'm a client and nothing fucking else. And if I did want to start something with her... it would be dangerous for her. I have a lot of fucking enemies, and I don't want the waitress's blood on my hands.

Right now, though, her blood is the least of my problems. I'm more worried about my own. About the fact that my cock is swollen, ready to fucking burst with the weight of cum in my balls. I want to spill it all over her. I want to watch her wake up and realize she's soaked in my fucking seed.

The thought consumes me, and I grit my teeth, jerking my cock, fast and relentless. I'm getting harder, the veins of my cock angrily pulsing with blood and unspilled seed.

My mind is racing. I don't let shit like this happen. I don't get hard-ons for little sluts who'll suck anybody's cock for a couple of hundred bucks. Yet I'm fucking enthralled, enticed by this vixen.

"Fuck," I mutter again. "Fuck, sugar."

My motions become faster. I stroke myself, bringing myself closer to an inescapable orgasm. I know I'm going to fucking come before it even happens. And the moment it does, I stop fucking holding back.

Positioning my cock over Monroe's sleeping form, I jerk myself faster and fucking faster. With a groan, I massage the tip of my cock right over her face. Just inches away from her parted, sweet mouth.

The first rope of cum is unexpected. It spurts out, landing on Monroe's innocent face. She stirs in her sleep but doesn't wake up.

I keep fucking jerking because it's too late to stop now. I'm too far fucking gone.

Monroe's tongue darts out between her lips. In her sleep, she lets out the smallest of moans and licks the droplets of cum from her mouth. I groan and keep fucking jerking. Another rope of cum spurts from my tip, landing on her shirt. Then more on her thighs. I position my cock so it goes all over her, licking my lips and fighting the urge to wake her up and make her clean herself while I continue to stroke myself.

I'm in-fucking-satiable.

And my phone's going off again.

With a hissed curse on my lips, I pull out my lit-up cell. A restricted number. Fuck.

I have to go. I have work to do. When the Lombardis need a kill, this is how they get in contact. Soon enough, I'll get a text in code with my victim and location. I haven't prepared for this because it's supposed to be my night off. Yet I can't say no, not to these men.

Looking around the room, I spot a mirror above Monroe's dresser with her makeup lined up under it. I grab a lipstick, unscrew it, and write her a message on the mirror.

I'll be watching you. -A

Taking a step back, I admire my work. She'll be so fucking scared when she wakes up covered in my seed with that cryptic message on the mirror. I wish I could be around to see the fear in her eyes as she comes to the realization I did this. I'm the one fucking with her. I'm the one she should be afraid of.

I make sure everything's as it was when I came in. I walk back to my car and take off my black leather gloves. I switch from feeling like a horny teenager to the ruthless murder machine my employers expect me to be.

Someone's going to die tonight.

I'll take special pleasure in watching their blood spurt, coloring the walls dark red.

It'll be like therapy. Therapy for my fucked-up heart that wants nothing more than to go back inside that cramped apartment, put my hand over Monroe's mouth, and fuck her senseless. Therapy for my black fucking heart that bleeds when I see girls like her, girls with a bright future, selling their perfect bodies for a couple of thousand.

The world's a sick fucking place.

And I'm only making it worse.

4
MONROE

I wake up with the oddest feeling. It's like a sixth sense telling me that something is not right. I open my eyes and stare at the familiar white ceiling of my bedroom. A brown water stain is the only thing standing out, but that's been there since I moved in.

Frowning, I push the thin blanket off my body. Cool air washes over my heated skin, and that's when I feel it. Something is on my face. My hand flies to my cheek to touch the spot. I run my fingers over the dried substance that's caked onto my face.

What the hell?

I sit up in haste, eager to figure out what this stuff could be. My eyes fall onto the mirror sitting on my dresser, and my heart stops when I read the words.

I'll be watching you. -A

I gape at the bright red lettering covering my mirror. Blinking slowly, I hope that they will somehow disappear each time I close my eyes. I must be dreaming. Yes, I'm still asleep.

Only, I've never felt like this in a dream before. I've never felt this kind of terror, no matter how bad the nightmare got. My heart has started beating again, but it settles in an unnaturally fast rhythm, pumping adrenaline through my veins.

My gaze zeros in on the A it's been signed with. I know right away who he is. The man from the club. I don't know how or why, but I know it's him. He found me.

Frantically, I scan the room, half expecting him to jump out from the closet any minute. Oh my god, what if he's still here?

I briefly entertain the thought of calling the cops, but then I remember what Lucian said. The guy is in the mob. I don't know much about the mob, but if every movie I ever watched about organized crime is true, they have people from the police department on their payroll.

Pushing myself off the bed, I stand on unsteady feet and look around for a weapon. The lamp on my nightstand is small and made of cheap plastic, but the hardcover romance novel is thick and heavy. I grab it with both hands and hold it above my head, ready to throw it at the intruder.

On tiptoes, I sneak across the room, inching my way toward the open door. I come to a stop next to the dresser when I catch my reflection in the mirror. The dried substance on my face is a creamy white, and only then does my brain connect the dots.

It's cum. He fucking came on my face while I was sleeping.

The pure shock has the book slipping from my hands and landing on the floor with a loud thud. Startled, I jump half a foot in the air before spinning around like a maniac. My pulse is racing as I ready myself for some kind of attack.

When nothing happens after a few moments, I relax slightly, but not enough for my ragged breathing to even out. My whole body is tense as I make my way through the rest of the apartment, checking inside every closet and around every corner for him.

Only when I'm one-hundred-percent sure that I am alone do I sigh in relief. He is gone, at least for now.

Taking a butcher's knife from the kitchen —just in case— I lock myself in my bathroom. As I strip out of my nightshirt, I notice more dried cum on the fabric and my thigh. Jesus, did he do this more than once, and how in the world did I not wake up?

Turning on the shower, I let the water turn hot before stepping under the spray. As I scrub my body of the evidence of his visit, I keep my eyes trained on the knife lying on the counter within reaching distance. I scrub until my skin feels raw, but I still don't feel clean.

I give up when the water runs cold and the shivering gets to be too much. By the time I get out and dry off, my teeth are rattling together, threatening to crack my molars.

In record time, I get dressed and ready. Not bothering with makeup, I grab my phone, purse, and keys on my way out the door. There is only one place I'll feel safe right now. Even if it's just for a few hours. I need to feel safe, need to shove this mind-altering fear aside so I can think about what to do next.

I take three different buses to get to the Haven Senior Center. I might be paranoid, but the last thing I want is to lead a psycho to my grandma.

Doris from the front desk greets me with a smile, completely oblivious to the disturbing things going on inside my mind at the moment. Rushing past her, I head for the stairs, taking two steps at a time until I'm on the second floor.

My grandma's room is the last one at the end of the hall. For every two steps I take, I sneak a quick glance over my shoulder to make sure no one is following me. The hallway remains empty as I stand in front of my grandma's door for a moment to gather myself. I don't want her to realize something is wrong.

Taking a deep, calming breath, I lift my hand and gently rap my knuckles over the smooth wood.

"Come in," her muffled voice yells through the door a second after my knock.

Turning the brass knob, I push the door open and step inside. The familiar scent of fresh linen and lavender fills my senses, putting me at ease right away.

"Well, hello dear," Grandma's sing-song voice meets my ear and another wave of calm washes over me. She is sitting close to the window, the rays of sunshine turning her gray hair shiny like silver. A book is perched in her lap, and a steaming hot cup of coffee sits on the side table next to her.

"Hi, Grams," I greet her, closing the door behind me. I set my purse on the floor next to the door and move in to give my grandma a hug. Leaning down to where she's sitting in her wheelchair, I wrap my arms around her shoulders and hold her close.

"You're early today. Is everything okay?" she asks when I release her reluctantly.

"Yes, just wanted to see you. You know, spend some more time with you. I don't have to work until later tonight."

"I wish you wouldn't work at a bar. It's not safe for a beautiful woman like yourself."

It's not the first time she has voiced her concerns, but they were always invalid. Lucian treats his staff well and never forces anyone to do something they don't want to. I always felt protected there... until now.

"I'm fine, I promise." I hate lying to her, but I can't stand her worrying sick, and I really need the money, which is another thing I'm lying to her about. She has no idea how expensive this place really is, and I'm going to keep it this way. She wouldn't be okay with me spending nine hundred dollars a week on this place. On the other hand, I would pay even more to ensure she's taken care of the way she deserves.

"Are you sure, dear? You look a bit pale—"

"Why don't we take a walk through the garden?" I cut her off, trying desperately to distract her.

"Are you sure?" she asks, inspecting my face like she is trying to solve a puzzle. "I guess some fresh air would be nice."

"Great." I clap my hands together in fake excitement before starting to push Grams out the door and down the hall.

Passing the staircase, I head to the elevators and push the call button. The door slides open with a ping, and I am left staring into the small space ahead of me. My stomach is in knots. I hate this part.

Without actually going into the elevator, I extend my arms to push my grandma inside to where she can reach the buttons.

"I'll meet you downstairs." Luckily, I don't have to explain myself. This is the way we do it every time. I help her into the elevator, and then I'll take the stairs. My fear of confined spaces is simply too strong, and she understands that, knowing exactly why I'm this way.

By the time I get downstairs, she has already arrived and is wheeling herself out. I meet her in the foyer and take over pushing so she can relax.

We walk through the garden for a long time. She tells me about dinner and the show the center put on for the seniors last night. Then she goes on about the book she's been reading, and in return, I tell her about the one I recently picked up from the library.

We grab some lunch and drink coffee on the terrace after. Everything around me, all worry and fear, just disappears when I'm with her. That's why I'm not surprised when I suddenly realize it's getting dark outside.

"Shit, I'm gonna miss the bus if I don't leave like… now. Ugh, sorry, Grams. I have to rush out."

"Don't worry, hun. Thanks for spending the day with me."

I give her one last kiss on the cheek before I dash out the door and down the stairs. I make it around the corner just in time to see the bus take off without me in it.

Shit!

Frustrated, I grab the handle on my purse tighter as if strangling the fake leather will resolve all my problems. I could call a cab, but I've just caught up with all the bills for the first time in months. I can't start spending cash to fix my own carelessness.

Thankfully, I chose my comfortable sneakers this morning. I march down the sidewalk while keeping a fast pace. The sun is almost down all the way now, the streetlights providing most of the light. The air turns frigid swiftly, and I wrap my arms around myself as I walk.

It isn't long before I regret my choice. Every sound I hear startles me, every car passing by causes my pulse to spike, and every dark corner I see freaks me out a little more.

I tell myself it's all in my head… until it's not.

Everything happens so fast. Cruel hands come out of nowhere. Meaty fingers dig into my skin with bruising force as two men drag me into an alley.

I open my mouth to scream, but before any sound comes out, a large hand covers my mouth. The smell of dirt, urine, and cheap alcohol fills my nostrils. A combination that has bile rise in my throat.

"Who do we have here?" One of my attackers chuckles. "Walking around the city all alone after dark. You're basically asking to have your cunt filled."

"And the ass." The other guy grins, showing off half of his front teeth missing. "Don't forget the ass, Chuck."

One of them forcefully grabs a handful of my breast while another kneads my butt cheek through my thin dress. I flail my arms and kick my leg out, earning me a slap in the face. My cheek stings, and tears start to run down my face as I desperately try to fight these two men off.

"We're going to have so much fun with you—" His words are cut off as his body is flung backward as though he weighs hardly anything. A dark figure appears in front of us, his face nothing but a mask of fury, almost unrecognizable… almost.

The guy behind me releases his hold on me, and I stumble away from the three men.

"Hey, man, we don't want any trouble with you people." One of my assailants holds up his hands in surrender.

"Shut up," A growls at him, like I imagine a feral animal would at his prey.

"We didn't know she was—" He chokes on his words when he catches sight of the murderous look in A's eyes.

Fuck, fuck, fuck… the word runs on replay through my mind. Fuck, he's going to kill them. And he's not going to let me walk away. At that exact moment, I know my life is over.

I'm going to die.

5

ALARIC

I make quick work of the two bastards who dragged her into the alley. I don't even use a gun. With a painful-sounding crunch, I break the first one's neck. His useless body drops to the ground, hitting it with a thud.

The other guy looks for a way to escape, but it's too fucking late. Before he can make a run for it, I grab him by the throat and slam him against the wall in the alley.

"Please, man," he grunts, his voice raspy since I'm squeezing his worthless throat so fucking hard. "Have mercy, I didn't know she was your girl."

"Too fucking late," I grind out, snapping his neck, too. His body falls to the ground like a useless, broken puppet. And now it's just me and Monroe, who's shivering behind me.

Slowly, I turn around to face her. At least there's no fucking blood. I leave the bodies there, grab her arm, and drag her out of the alley.

"What are you doing?" she whispers, her voice trembling. "I can't believe you—"

"Shut up." I keep pulling her along until we're a street over. Then I drag her into another alley and press her back against the wall. "What the fuck are you doing, walking around alone like that?"

"Are you actually making this my fault right now?" she hisses, narrowing her eyes at me. "I was just trying to get home! And what the hell are you doing here, anyway?"

"Keeping an eye on you," I grunt. "Good thing I am, since you don't have a fucking clue how to look out for your own ass."

Her eyes burn with anger. "You killed them. Oh God, you fucking killed them."

"Shut up," I repeat. "You'll get us in trouble."

"Oh God, oh God, oh God." Her eyes are growing wider and wider, and her pupils have dilated so much her pretty eyes look nearly black. "I can't believe it. I just saw two men die. For nothing."

"They would've hurt you." I put my hand on the brick wall behind her, and she turns her head to the side, closing her eyes so she doesn't have to look at me. "They would've raped you. Or worse. Shouldn't you be fucking thanking me?"

"You're a monster." Her words are barely above a whisper now. "Fuck. They're dead because of me."

"They're dead because they were assaulting an innocent girl. There are rules at play here, sugar. They should never have touched you. Because you're mine."

"Just because you're stalking me doesn't make me your property." She punctuates her words by pushing a finger into my chest.

"You're fucking crazy, *A*. I know you were in my apartment last night."

"Oh, you do?" I smirk at her. "Got any way to prove it?"

She peels her back away from the wall and advances on me, but I don't move. She seems intimidated, but she stands her ground. It's actually kind of fucking cute.

"You *came* on me, you pervert," she hisses. "I was covered in it this morning. And your message is still on my mirror."

"You have no way to prove it."

"I'm sure there are fingerprints all over my fucking room," she snaps, but all I do is flash her my hands in my signature black leather gloves. She pales, her bottom lip trembling. "You got nothing on me, sugar. But you're right about one thing. You've seen me kill now. You're a liability."

She looks shocked and afraid as I grab her forearm. "Don't kill me."

"Why shouldn't I?" I bark. Even though I have no intention of harming the barely legal waitress, this is giving me a hard-on. I love the fear in her eyes. It's fucking exciting.

"Because I..." She blanches, shakily tucking a strand of hair behind her ear. "I have to... I have to..."

"Great reasons, sugar," I hiss. "I'm not going to kill you. But you are coming with me."

"What? Where?" She resists. "Let me go."

"We can do this the easy way or the hard way, sugar. You fight me, I'll put a knife to your throat and walk you to my goddamn car. Or you can come willingly."

"I'm not going anywhere with you," she spits out. "Don't you think someone will call the cops if you drag me through the street with a knife pressed to my neck?"

"See this?" I flash her the red ribbon on my wrist. "Nobody will fuck with me. Not even the police. Now come the fuck on."

She doesn't argue, but I can see the trace of tears in her eyes. Ignoring it, I make her walk ahead of me. Two blocks go by. People see us and avert their eyes when I flash them the ribbon on my wrist. No one's going to help Monroe, not when I'm with her.

We reach my car, and her eyes widen when she sees it. I put her in the back seat and make quick work of tying her up with the seat belt.

"Are you serious?" Monroe growls.

"Very." I tighten the seat belt so she's immobilized. "I'm not risking you attacking me while I drive. Now be a good girl and shut the fuck up so I can fucking think."

I get into the driver's seat. I don't have to think about where I'm taking her because I already know where I want her. In my house, on my bed, with her legs spread and my seed dripping out of that delicious little cunt I haven't tasted yet. Revving the engine, I start driving.

Every so often, I check on Monroe in the rear-view mirror. Her eyes are open, and tears are sliding down her cheeks. If I didn't have a black fucking heart, I'd actually feel sorry for her. But I'm ruthless. A killer. I wanted her, so I'm fucking taking her. It's not like she'll be missing out. Her life seems pretty fucking shitty, so I'll give her a better one. I'll make her appreciate me.

The short drive to my house is charged with tension. I pull up in front of my house, and Monroe closes her eyes so she doesn't have to see where I've brought her. I kill the engine after parking in the garage and take a deep breath, trying to figure out how the fuck I'm going to handle this.

I don't have a room to put her in. All this has happened too fast, and I'm not fucking prepared for it. Until I figure this shit out, I'll just have to improvise.

I get out of the car and open the back door to find her glaring at me, eyes filled with contempt. "Are you going to be a good girl, or are you going to make this difficult for yourself?"

She doesn't reply. Just keeps staring daggers at me in return, which only makes me smirk.

"Ah, the silent treatment. So fucking original, sugar. Come on, we're going."

I undo the seat belts holding her in place and help her get up. She doesn't fight me, but she is fucking shaking, and her fear excites me. I march her into the house. If she's surprised by how beautiful, expensive, and modern my home is, she doesn't show it. She just keeps walking until we reach the bedroom.

"Get on the bed," I hiss.

"Why?" she snaps. "So you can fucking *rape* me?"

"Keep dreaming. On the bed. Now."

Sullenly, she gets up on the bed, and I open the nightstand to grab a pair of handcuffs. I attach one to her wrist and the other to the railing of the bed.

"Don't do this," she says softly as the handcuffs click shut. "Don't leave me here. I have... I have things and people I love out there. Don't keep me here."

"You give me no choice, sugar."

"I won't tell anyone," she rushes to say. "I won't tell anyone you killed those men. Just let me go."

"I can't," I mutter, running a finger over her cheek. She flinches when I do it. I should feel like a bastard for doing this shit to her, but I'm just getting fucking excited. My cock strains against my pants, eager to break through the fabric and bury itself in her throat. But I fight my instincts the best I fucking can. "Are you afraid of me?"

"Yes," she replies instantly. "I don't trust you."

"I'm not going to hurt you. Not unless you ask for it."

"I'll never do that," Monroe hisses, making me smirk.

"We'll see. We're going to stay here tonight because I need to keep an eye on you. When you want to use the bathroom, you say so. Got it?"

She nods, her lips pressed together. "I'm thirsty."

I get her a glass of water and some fruit. When I get back, I sit down on the edge of the bed. Monroe stares ahead. Instead of simply handing her the water, I open the bottle for her, then hold it to her lips. She takes a few large gulps before turning her head slightly, signaling she is done.

Setting down the bottle, I pick up a piece of strawberry and hold it in front of her mouth, which pulls into a frown. "I can feed myself."

"I know you can, but I'm going to do it. Open up."

She huffs out in annoyance but opens her mouth regardless. I smirk, knowing she is trying to do it in the least sexy way possible. She simply laxes her jaw and sticks her tongue out like a sulking child. I find it adorable.

I set the strawberry on her tongue, making sure both my index finger and thumb touch the inside of her mouth as I do. I pull my hand away slowly, and her lips close, catching the tip of my index finger and sucking it back into her mouth.

My dick twitches, and I wish it was my cock back in her mouth. That is, until the moment her teeth sink into my flesh. She bites down on my finger, making me hiss out in pain.

In a split second, my free hand is wrapped around her throat. Her mouth flies open with a scream, releasing my finger. I don't squeeze her neck. I simply hold her in place, making sure she knows who's in charge.

"I'm sorry!" She apologizes quickly, all her sassiness replaced by fear.

"What am I going to do with you, Monroe?" I keep my fingers around her throat loosely, running my thumb over her jugular where I can feel her heart beating furiously. "I'm going to feed you the rest, and you are going to eat every bit I give you. Understood?"

She nods, and I release her. I feed her the fruit, and she takes every bit without another word. I wipe the red juice of the strawberries from the corner of her lips. Her eyes meet mine.

"I don't want to die."

"I'm not going to kill you, Monroe. But I need to figure this shit out. And if my employer finds out what I've done, you're fucking dead already."

She leans against the pillows, closing her eyes. A flash of guilt stabs through me, reminding me that I'm human after all. But as fast as it appears, it drifts off into nothing. Monroe's dress is riding up, and I can see her panties. I can see the wet spot in front of them. I reach forward, and she protests with a gasp as I rub my thumb over the front of them.

"Why are you fucking wet, sugar?"

"I..." She swallows her reply, glaring at me. "I don't know."

"Is this turning you on?"

"No!" She glares at me, her eyes shooting daggers. "I hate you."

"I'm sure you fucking do. Is that why you're wet?"

"I'm not," she hisses, and I laugh out loud, swiping my fingers between her legs. They come away wet.

"So this isn't real?" I ask her, licking my fingers. "Who are you dripping for, sugar?"

"Not you."

"Oh, no? Then who? The bad men in the alley?"

"Fuck you." Her eyes shoot daggers at me. I've pissed her off now. "I don't get wet for killers."

"You keep lying to yourself, sugar." I reach between her legs and push her panties to the side. Her soaked pussy looks so fucking tempting that I groan as I swipe my fingers between her lips. "See this? This is for me. You're wet for me. Ready for me. Even though you say you don't want it, your body is fucking begging for it."

She grits her teeth together, refusing to reply. I push my fingers between her lips, and she fights back a moan. She is so fucking tight, I can barely move my finger in and out. Tight enough to be... I pull them back and glare at her. "Are you fucking kidding me, Monroe?"

"What?"

"Are you a goddamn virgin?"

"What? No, of course not," she snaps. "Why would you think that? And why would it matter anyway?"

"It matters because I don't want some prudish little girl," I growl. I can't do what I'm planning to do to a virgin.

"Do you really think a virgin would work at Purgatory?" She rolls her eyes at me.

"I guess not," I say, calming myself a bit more. I near her again and gently wipe her tears from her face. She keeps glaring at me. "You've had a long fucking day. You should get some rest."

"Handcuffed to your bed?"

"If you behave like a good girl, I'll give you more freedom."

"Great," she spits out, closing her eyes. Her body is wracked by sobs then. Soft whimpers escape her lips, and she stops caring. I watch her cry.

She's hiding something. I'll get it out of her soon enough. But not today. Today, Monroe needs to be comforted. Something that's fucking alien to me. Yet seeing her like this makes me want to learn how to help her.

Frustrated, I walk out of the room and slam the door shut. Leaning against it, I try to come to terms with everything that's happened.

There's an innocent girl handcuffed to my bed. Even if she isn't a virgin, she is inexperienced, fucking naïve, and much too young for me.

Yet I already know I can't ever let her go.

6

MONROE

What the hell was I thinking? Why did I lie to him? I should have told him the truth that yes, I'm a fucking virgin. While my high school friends were going on dates and having sex, I spent my teenage years working and taking care of my grandma.

I have no idea what possessed me to lie, but the way he got mad about my possible innocence scared the shit out of me. He keeps saying he won't kill me, but how can I believe him? What if he is only keeping me alive for sex? That would be more likely than anything else.

All these unanswered questions are giving me a headache, or maybe it's the crying. I try to rub my forehead, forgetting I'm cuffed to the bed. The metal digs into my skin as I tug on it, causing me to yelp out in pain. *Fuck.*

Fresh tears fall down my cheek, soaking his crisp white pillow. I hope I at least leave a stain. It's a ridiculous thought, but somehow it calms me a little. If I leave a stain, he'll have to wash it, and imagining him doing the laundry makes him seem a little less scary and more... normal.

I'm not sure how long I'm left alone in the bed, but it feels like a long time. I'm exhausted, and my head hurts, but I still can't go to sleep. My eyes won't stay closed.

Just as the first morning light filters through the curtains, the door opens, and A's huge form enters the room. I try to sit up as much as I can, feeling a bit safer that way. Of course I know that's an illusion. I'm not in any less danger.

"Did you not sleep any?"

"It's a little hard to get comfortable being cuffed to the bed of the person I watched kill two people hours ago."

Frowning at my answer, he reaches for something in his back pocket, and I immediately regret my mouthing off. A scream builds in my throat, but then I realize he only grabbed the key.

"I'm going to uncuff you, and then we're both going to lie down and go to sleep," he tells me while reaching for the cuffs. The click of the lock meets my ear, and then I'm free.

Pulling my arms down, I rub at my shoulders to alleviate the soreness from having been raised for so long. He undresses, and no matter how much I tell myself to look away, my gaze stays glued to him. His body is a work of art—his muscular form covered in ink and scars that tell a story of a savage life.

"I was only going to sleep, but if you keep looking at me like that, we're going to do more than that," A warns, and I avert my vision to the ceiling, making him chuckle.

A moment later, the mattress dips, and he moves to lie beside me. I'm still staring at the ceiling when his arm wraps around my body, and he pulls me into his. My back is against his chest, his body wrapped around mine like a blanket. I want to object... should object, but he is so warm, and his skin on mine feels so good.

"Sleep," he whispers into the shell of my ear, and against all odds, I do.

~

I WAKE up with something heavy draped over my middle, pushing me down into the most comfortable mattress I've ever slept on.

Opening my eyes, I feel nothing but disappointed in myself. Bright light is coming through the window, filling every corner of the room. How could I have slept through the night? In his bed. With him next to me. I'm still shocked that he left me uncuffed during the night, but then again, he is holding on to me like a bear holds a salmon.

Cursing myself, I force my breathing to remain even while I listen intently, trying to figure out if A is still sleeping. When I hear nothing but his heavy breath, I decide to take my chance. Ever so slowly, I wiggle my way out of his arm and off the mattress.

My bare feet make contact with the cool hardwood floor before I sneak a peek over my shoulder. A's eyes are closed, and his face remains lax.

On gentle feet, I start tiptoeing around the room, grabbing shoes off the floor as I head toward the door. My fingertips graze the metal doorknob when his deep voice booms through the room.

"Going somewhere?"

I pull my hand away from the knob like it suddenly bursts into flames. Spinning around while clutching the dress to my chest, I stare at A's scowling at me from the bed. Lifting his finger, he motions for me to come back to bed.

Sighing in defeat, I drop my clothes and walk back to the bed with my head hanging low. "You can't expect me not to try."

"I expect you not to succeed, for your own sake."

"You can't just keep me here."

"I can, and I will. The pleasantness of your stay with me is entirely up to you, but I can promise you one thing. If you try to leave again, I will kill you."

I swallow. Hard. He's not joking. The death glare he gives me right now leaves no room for a misunderstanding. If I don't listen, he'll kill me.

"I need money," I blurt out.

He cocks his head at me, inspecting me curiously. "Money? I just gave you a bunch. What did you do with that cash?"

"I paid off some debt and a few bills ahead," I say truthfully. "But more bills are going to pile up soon, and I can't not pay them."

"What kind of bills?"

"My apartment for one, my phone and power bill…" I trail off. There is really not much more besides Grams's facility, but I'm not ready to tell him about that.

"You won't need any of that since you are staying here. Tell me the real reason you need that money. Are you sending it to someone?"

"I just need it, okay? You want to keep me as your live-in sex toy? Fine, pay me. I want nine hundred dollars a week. You can do whatever you want to me for that."

Excitement glistens in his eyes, and I'm already certain he is going to take the deal. "Why not just keep you and force you to be my sex toy for free?"

"Because I know you'd rather have me cooperate." *At least I hope.* He killed the two guys for almost raping me, so I am going out on a limb and saying he doesn't want to force me.

"Fine, I'll give you nine hundred a week, but let's get two things straight. One, I still don't trust you. Two, I get to do whatever I want, which is going to be a very specific fantasy of mine." A smile tugs on his lips, but his eyes are anything but friendly. They promise something dark.

"L-like what?" I remember him having me in the BDSM room and not being interested in any of the toys there. I know what people do in the other rooms upstairs, and none of that scares me. It's the stuff they do downstairs that has my skin crawling. "Are you going to hurt me?"

"No," he says right away, and a weight—one I didn't even know was there— is lifted from my chest. "What I have planned won't hurt you, but it is a bit unorthodox."

"You won't tell me what it is?"

"No. I'd rather it be a surprise." He kicks off the blanket and gets out of the bed. My eyes fall onto his almost naked body. He is only wearing a pair of black boxers, the rest of his muscular body on full display.

"If you won't tell me that, will you at least tell me your name?"

"Alaric."

Alaric. I try the name out in my head. It's stupid, but I'm a little less scared of him now that I know his name. It makes him a little less mysterious and a little more human.

"Come on, let's take a shower." Alaric motions for me to enter the attached bathroom.

"Together?" I ask as if I don't already know the answer.

"Yes." He smirks.

I step into the bathroom, suddenly feeling a bit shy, which is stupid, considering what I just agreed on doing. Besides, he already saw me completely naked at the club.

"Take your shirt and panties off," he orders while ridding himself of his own underwear. I watch his already hard cock spring free, and my mouth waters as the memory of that thing in my mouth resurfaces.

Grabbing the hem of the shirt I slept in, I pull it over my head, realizing how tight and sensitive my nipples feel. He turns on the shower while keeping his eyes trained on me as I push down my panties next.

The large shower is made for at least two people, but as I step inside with Alaric, it feels small and cramped. If it wasn't for the shower walls being made of glass, I would surely have a panic attack right about now.

Intricate mosaic tiles line the inside of the shower, but I have a hard time appreciating it at the moment. I'm too busy eyeing the man in front of me. He is a good foot taller than me, his chest so large it seems like it's permanently puffed out. His upper arms are the size of my thighs, and his hands could easily wrap around my entire throat.

Uncertainty worms its way through my body. Did I just make a deal with the devil? He said he wouldn't hurt me, but can I believe him? Can I trust him so easily?

"Get the washcloth and put some soap on it. I want you to wash me." I stare at the washcloth hanging on a hook like it's a foreign object. "All of me," he specifies.

Nodding, I take the cloth and squirt some soap on it like instructed. The fresh masculine scent fills my nose as I tentatively bring the rag to Alaric's stomach and start to rub it over his skin. Soap bubbles form as I drag it up across his hair-covered chest and over his shoulders while the running water washes it away almost immediately.

"Is this your kink? Me washing you?"

"No." The sound of his deep laughter echoing around the room takes me by surprise. "Not that, but I do like your hands on me."

Besides the occasional muscle twitching, he stands completely still while I wash his entire upper body. That changes as soon as I lower myself to my knees. I look up at him through my lashes and notice his chest puffing up, making him look impossibly big. I feel like a dwarf in front of a giant, hoping not to get crushed.

While on my knees, I tentatively start running the cloth over each of his legs. His large thighs flex every time I get even close to his cock, which I'm definitely saving for last. After both of his legs, I reach around and do his taut ass cheeks. He groans, the sounds vibrating through my body, and I can't help imagining what his ass looks like while he takes me.

I shut down my dirty thoughts as my face turns red. I drop the washcloth to the ground, knowing I won't need it for what's to come next.

My eyes finally land on the iron rod between his legs, which I have been trying to avoid. It looks painfully swollen, making me feel a little guilty that I haven't helped him relieve this.

"I want you to jerk me off, and when I'm ready to come, you're going to close your eyes and open your mouth so I can come all over your pretty face."

Swallowing hard, I nod slightly and follow his command. I wrap my small hand around his swollen shaft and start to stroke up and down his length. He groans and thrusts his hips into my hand so slightly, I'm not sure he is aware of doing it.

"Do you even know how hard you make me? Pretending you don't know what you are doing. Use both hands, sugar. Jerk me like you mean it."

Again, I do what he says. Using both of my hands, I stroke him hard. His groans get louder, and his body starts twitching while my knees are aching and my arms are starting to get tired.

"Fuck. I'm already ready to come. Close your eyes, open your mouth, and stick your tongue out," he orders, and I obey.

A moment later, his cock swells in my hands. He stills, and ropes of sticky cum hit my face. Some gets into my mouth, making me cringe at the salty taste it leaves on my tongue.

"Swallow it," he demands, his voice rough and gravelly. "Then lick my cock clean."

Without questioning him, I swallow, then stick my tongue out and run it over his skin, licking him clean of the leftover cum.

A small voice in the back of my head tells me what I'm doing is wrong. I shouldn't let him boss me around like this. But then there's this other voice, the more depraved part of me, that knows this is exactly what I want. I want him to take control, to tell me what to do. I want to please him.

"Good girl," Alaric praises as I get back on my feet. "I'd like to do the same for you right now, but unfortunately, that will have to wait. I have somewhere to go, and if I start eating that sweet pussy of yours now, I know I'll miss my meeting."

I try to hide my disappointment, but the deep chuckle coming from him tells me I wasn't able to. I quickly wash my hair and body before rinsing off. Alaric steps out of the shower and dries himself off. When I step out, he holds up a fluffy white towel to wrap me up in.

Back in the bedroom, he gives me another clean oversized shirt and a pair of sweatpants. While I roll the waistband five times, he gets into a black button-up shirt and a charcoal suit. Curiosity has a question on the tip of my tongue, but I know better than to ask him where he's going.

"Let's get you something to eat really quick." He takes my hand and leads me into the kitchen where he gets out some granola bars, a protein shake, and a bottle of water. "I don't really have anything else here, but I'll bring some lunch."

"This is fine," I tell him, not wanting to mention that this is better than what I usually eat for breakfast.

"All right, back this way," he tells me, carrying the food and drinks. I'm a little confused when he leads me back to the bedroom and dumps everything on the bed. He goes to the nightstand and pulls out the handcuffs from yesterday.

"You don't have to do that. I told you I'll cooperate."

"And I told you that I don't trust you yet. So either you can get on the bed so I can cuff you, or I'll lock you in the trunk of my car while I'm at my meeting."

I basically jump onto the bed at the mere thought of being locked in a small and dark space. Alaric gives me a curious look, raising his eyebrow in question like he is trying to solve a puzzle. Thankfully, he doesn't comment because I'm not about to explain that part of myself.

"I won't be long," he promises as he cuffs my wrist to the iron bar on his headboard. As soon as he's done, he turns away from me and leaves the room without another glance back. It's almost like he can't get away quick enough.

The question is, is he hurrying away because he has to or because he wants to?

7

ALARIC

It didn't take me long to figure out why Monroe asks for nine hundred dollars specifically. After I checked out the senior home I watched her visit the other day, a simple look at their website told me that this is the cost for someone to stay there. So she lied to me about her family. She must have someone in there she loves, someone she is willing to spend her entire paycheck for.

I can't even imagine loving someone so much. To stay in that shitty place she lives in, work at Purgatory, and whatever else shit she's doing. The way she begged for money the first night we met is put in a whole new light now because she didn't beg for herself. She begs for someone she cares for.

She is selfless, innocent, and so fucking sweet. She couldn't be any more of my opposite. Maybe that's why I'm so drawn to her—opposites attract and all.

After a quick morning meeting with my boss, I drive back to my house in a hurry, knowing she's tied to my bed. If she hadn't already made me come earlier today to take the edge off, I would probably be jerking off in the car right now. Fuck, this woman is driving me insane.

I pull into my garage and kill the engine. The garage door hasn't even come down all the way before I grab the bag of takeout from the passenger seat and head inside the house. I set the bag of food on the kitchen table and speed walk to the bedroom.

I open the door and find her on the bed just as I left her. She's awake, glaring at me with the cutest pout on her face.

"Miss me?" I ask with a grin. She basically scoffs at me, making me smile even wider.

"The only thing I miss is not being tied up."

"I'll undo your cuffs soon but not just yet. First, I'm going to return the favor," I tell her as I slip out of my shoes and climb on to the bed.

She jerks away from me, crawling up the bed as much as she can with her hands tied to the headboard. "What are you doing?"

"I told you. I'm returning the favor." Grabbing her ankle, I pull her toward me so she's flat on her back again. A shocked yelp falls from her lips, and I grasp her other ankle before she can even think about kicking me.

"You don't have to do this." She tries to wiggle out of my hold, but I still manage to tug my sweatpants off her legs.

"I know." Grabbing her knees, I spread her open for me and move between her thighs. "But I really want to."

She starts to say something else, probably arguing with me about not doing this, but her words are cut off when I lower my head and bury my face in her pussy.

I run my tongue right through her slit, and we both moan in unison. Digging my fingers into her thighs to keep her legs spread, I devour her like a starving man.

I lick, suck, and nibble on her clit until she wiggles beneath me, lifting her hips to get closer to my face. I peek over her flat stomach and between her breasts to see her expression.

Her eyes are closed, and her lips are parted. Her chest heaves, and her hands are wrapped around the headboard rails as if she needs something to hold on to.

Running my tongue down her slit, I dip it into her cunt, drawing another moan from her lips. She is so fucking tight that even my tongue won't go in far.

Her thighs quiver around my shoulders, and I know she's going to come soon. I go back to the small bundle of nerves and give it my full attention, circling my tongue around it before sucking hard.

Her back arches off the bed as she falls apart. Her body tightens, and she tries to close her thighs as her release coats my tongue. I keep her spread open so I can lick her pussy clean. I want every drop.

After her moment, her body goes slack, but she continues to breathe heavily as if she just ran a marathon. I sit up so I can take in her sated body. Her pussy is glistening with wetness, and her clit is red and swollen. I can't wait to finally fuck her. *Soon...*

Her face is flushed, and her eyes are still closed as she's trying to catch her breath, but they fly open when I start moving off the bed. She watches me with hooded eyes while I take out the key from my pocket and unlock her cuffs.

Silently, she rubs at her wrists and closes her legs like she's suddenly feeling shy.

"Come on, I got us some lunch. I just wanted to eat my dessert first." I smirk, making her cheeks turn even redder.

I climb off the bed, adjusting my dick to get a little bit more comfortable. Monroe scurries off the bed too, grabbing her discarded sweatpants and putting them on in a hurry.

She goes to use the bathroom and wash up before I walk her to the dining room area. She takes a seat, and I enter the attached kitchen to grab two bottles of water and some silverware. My house has an open floor plan so I can watch her from anywhere in the living area.

"You can unwrap the food and see which one you like the best," I tell her as I take the seat next to her.

She peeks into the bag and grabs one of the sandwiches and a small bowl of soup. I hand her the spoon, and she digs in as soon as she pops the lid open.

I grab the remaining sandwich out of the bag and unwrap it. We both eat in silence, but I can't help watching her. Even the way she eats his fucking sexy. The way she wraps her lips around the spoon and the way her tongue darts out to lick the mayo from the corner of her mouth. Everything she does is driving me insane. I need to think about something else before I swipe the food off the table and fuck her senseless.

"Tell me about yourself. Why are you afraid of small spaces?"

She puts down the last bite of her sandwich. "I'm pretty sure everyone is afraid to be locked in a small, dark space."

"Probably yes, but I feel like it was more for you. You looked like you were about to have a panic attack just from me mentioning being locked in the trunk."

"How long am I supposed to stay here?" She obviously tries to change the subject. I let her get away with it for now, but I know there is more to the story, and I will know the answer eventually.

"How long?" She presses for an answer, so I give her one. The only one I can think of.

"Indefinitely."

8

MONROE

*I*ndefinitely? Did he just say *indefinitely*? He can't be serious. There is no way he expects me to stay here. My mouth opens to say something, but I can't think of an answer to that. What the hell do I tell him? A simple no is obviously not going to work with this man. So instead of saying anything, I simply sit there with my mouth hanging open like a fish out of water.

I'm so lost in my own head—trying to make sense of this situation I'm in—that I almost jerk myself off the chair when a loud ringing fills the room. I clutch my chest as my heart beats furiously against my rib cage in shock.

"It's just the doorbell. Calm down, sugar." Alaric gets up from the chair and pats my shoulder as he passes me.

Twisting in my chair, I follow Alaric with my eyes and watch him open the door as if he was expecting someone. An older man with gray hair matching his gray coat appears on the other side. A tight smile presses on his lips as Alarice waves him inside.

"Dr. Houseman, thank you for coming on such short notice."

Doctor?

I scan the man from head to toe. He is as tall as Alaric but is thin with lanky limbs instead. The pair of thick-rimmed glasses sitting on his nose seems slightly too large for his face. Besides his gray coat, he is dressed all in black. When he gets closer and turns slightly, I notice the leather bag he is carrying.

"Of course." The doctor gives him a quick nod before his eyes fall onto me. "This is my patient, I presume?" the man asks, pushing his glasses up his nose using his middle finger.

"Oh, no. No, I'm not sick," I blurt out.

"Where do you want me to set up?" Dr. Houseman asks, ignoring me completely.

"Right here in the living room will be fine. I just need you to take a few blood samples and administer some kind of birth control. No need for a full exam."

"Very well." He nods and walks into the living room area.

Blood samples? Birth control?

"I need you to go and sit on the couch. Let the doctor take some blood and choose birth control."

"Is that really necessary?" I ask even though I already know the answer. I don't even know why I'm fighting this other than I don't like that I'm forced to do it without him so much as telling me beforehand.

"Yes, this is necessary, and you will do this. Now be a good girl, and don't make me carry you over there."

A tiny part of me wants to tell him no, just to see how far I can push him, but the rest of me is way too nervous to even dare. Pushing myself off the chair, I stand on unsure legs and force them to carry me into the living room. Alaric follows close behind, which both calms and scares me. At least he can catch me if I pass out.

The doctor flips his bag open, and I can't help but inspect everything inside. Most of it looks like regular medical stuff—gauze, scissors, tape, alcohol wipes, and Band-Aids—but there are definitely things in there you can't find in a first-aid kit. A row of pill bottles and vials are lined up on one side, rolled-up tubing and an IV bag on the other.

"What exactly are we doing? I'm healthy, I promise."

The doctor glances over at Alaric as if to ask permission to talk to me at all. When Alaric gives him an approving nod, the doctor turns to me.

"I'm going to take some blood samples so I can test you for sexually transmitted diseases and other general health concerns."

"But I—" The words get stuck in my throat. I'm about to say I'm a virgin, but then I realize if I tell him now, that would change things drastically. The way I see it, two things could happen.

One, he's not going to believe me and think I'm a liar. Or two, he is going to ask the doctor to check if I truly am untouched. The thought of my stripping bare in front of these two men to spread my legs and have one probe into my vagina—doctor or not—causes my stomach to churn.

Then there is the after. If Alaric is certain I'm a virgin, he would not wait another day to have sex with me, and I still don't know what this kink of his is. All I know is that he won't take no for an answer if I don't like what he wants me to do. I might not have much of a choice in the end, but at least I can buy myself some time. So my smartest choice will be to just play along and let him think of me whatever he wants.

"Please, take a seat," the doctor nods to the spot in front of him while he lines up a few empty syringes and a needle head on a silver tray he pulled from his bag. "Lean back and relax."

I almost scoff at the word relax. As if.

I take a seat and fold my hands in my lap, waiting for him to put on a pair of latex gloves before I actually lean back into the soft cushion. He wraps a band tightly around my upper arm and turns it so the inside is up. After he thoroughly disinfects the skin where my arm bends, he uses his index finger to find a vein.

This isn't the first time I've had my blood taken, so I'm positively relieved when he finds a vein on the first try without having to dig the needle around. Quickly, three vials are filled with blood, and the needle is pulled from my arm. The doctor puts pressure on the tiny wound before simply putting a Band-Aid on it.

"I'll take this to the lab right away. Now let's talk about your birth control. Are you currently on anything?"

I simply shake my head.

"Have you ever taken anything in the past?" When I shake my head once more, he continues. "I recommend the Depo shot. It's very effective, and you don't have to worry about taking it every day."

Again, he turns to Alaric and asks him instead of me. "I have one with me today. I can give it to her now."

"Yes, go ahead," Alaric confirms without consulting me.

I feel like such a pushover for not even fighting him on this, but the truth is, I want this birth control as well. I'm way too young and broke to have a kid right now. The possibility of Alaric being the father seems like a terrible plan.

"This one will only be a small prick." He opens up another pack of disinfectant wipes and rubs the small pad against my upper arm, leaving a cold and tingling spot behind.

"When does she need her next shot?" Alaric asks.

"Every three months. I can send you a reminder message when it gets close to that time," the doctor tells him, and I almost laugh at the oddity of it all. He acts like he is running a normal practice when, in reality, nothing about this is *normal*.

He gives me the shot and starts gathering his things immediately after. I stay sitting on the couch, rubbing circles over the sore spot on my upper arm. At least there won't be any babies soon. Now I only have to convince Alaric to let me go.

"I'll call you as soon as I have the test results," the doctor tells Alaric as he sees him outside.

Once the door is closed and we are alone once more, Alaric comes to sit next to me. The couch dips under his weight, his muscle-clad frame leaning back casually.

"Tell me about yourself. How come you work at a place like Purgatory?" His question catches me off guard. Not because it's not a valid question, but the way he is asking me makes it seem like he actually cares to know.

"Um, Lucian pays well," I answer. It's not a lie either. Lucian pays an excellent salary, plus the tips are great, especially on the weekend.

"If the pay is so great, then why do you live in such a dump, and how did you accumulate so much debt?" he asks, an accusing note in the sound of his voice.

Shit. How am I going to get out of this without telling him about my grandma? He can't know about her. No one can know how much she means to me. I have to keep her safe.

"I grew up with a single mom," I whisper, staying as close to the truth as I can. "She was not great at managing finances or life in general. I had to figure out a lot on my own without guidance on top of her leaving me with a lot of baggage."

"No other family you're close with?" He raises an eyebrow, almost like he is daring me to lie.

Does he know about Grams? A sliver of fear crawls up my spine while I force the lie past my lips, "No, no one I'm close to."

He nods slightly, like he believes me, but the twinkle in his eyes makes me think the opposite. Either way, he doesn't press further.

"What about you?" I act casually. "Do you have a family you are close to?"

"No, not family by blood anyway." He points at the ribbon around his wrist. "The Lombardis are my family now. Took me in when I was sixteen, taught me everything I know. They are the only family I've known… at least until now."

Until now? I ignore his odd comment, having more pressing matters on my mind.

"But you kill people for them?" I don't know why I have to bring that fact up. I should have kept my mouth shut, especially considering what Alaric tells me next.

"Yes, I kill for them, but that's what I like to do. I enjoy killing other men, and I revel in the power it gives me. There is nothing that makes you feel more alive than snuffing the life out of someone else."

My eyes go wide, and blood freezes in my veins as I let his words sink in. He talks about taking a life as if it's a hobby of his, like another human soul doesn't matter to him the slightest.

"Don't worry, Monroe. I already told you, I won't kill you, but I can see your thoughts written all over your face. You don't have to fear me. The only people who have to worry are the people who try taking you away from me."

"I can't help but to be scared," I admit.

"I guess I'll have to try harder to prove it to you then."

Forcing a smile, I give him a slight nod. I wish my fear away as well, but I can't imagine a world where I wouldn't be terrified of a killer who enjoys death.

9

ALARIC

I'm enjoying having my little captive around. It's sure as hell managed to keep my cock hard every time I smell her scent in the hallway or catch a glimpse of her blond hair and pretty face. Her body is a distraction I didn't know I wanted, and I find myself readjusting my pants around her to hide my damn boner.

I can tell she still doesn't trust me, though. It's written all over her gorgeous face. And I fucking hate that somebody in her life must've let her down so badly that she still can't bring herself to trust.

I'm in my own bedroom tonight, tossing and turning when the urge to check in on her forces me to push my feet out from the duvet. I only have on a pair of pajama bottoms, my torso exposed, as I pad to her bedroom down the hall.

I open the door with a soft click, my eyes adjusting to the darkness. Walking up to the bed, I remember coming on her pretty little face that time in her apartment, and the same urge makes me push down the waistband of my pants and pull out my already throbbing cock.

But then I notice something in her expression that worries me. Her bottom lip is trembling, and she keeps shivering in the bed even though it's warm inside. Knitting my brows together, I cover my cock again and gently tuck away a curl from her forehead.

Her skin is slick with sweat, and it's obvious she's having a nightmare. I don't know *shit* about nightmares, but the way she's shaking and trembling makes me want to wake her up and tell her everything's okay.

I crawl into the bed and pull her trembling body against mine.

"Shh, it's okay," I mutter into her mass of hair, telling myself my vulnerability in this case doesn't matter. She's not even awake yet. She keeps shaking, her teeth chattering as I pull her on top of me. Finally, her eyes slowly open, and she mutters something I don't catch until she repeats it.

"Please, not again. Not again."

"It's okay." I pull more messy strands of hair off her face. "I'm here. You're safe. You were just having a bad dream."

"A...Alaric?" She rubs her eyes before settling against me. "What are you doing here?"

"I heard you crying out in your sleep."

"Liar." She grins at me, and I can't help but return the smile. "You were watching me sleep again, weren't you? Were you going to come on me again?"

"I guess you'll never know." I pull her against mine, nuzzling her hair. But then I remember who I'm supposed to be. A ruthless fucking killer. I shouldn't be doing this, shouldn't be getting attached. I pull back, and she thankfully doesn't seem to notice. "But you were having a nightmare, Monroe. A bad one."

"I know," she mutters, pulling away from me. I fight every instinct in me not to order her to stay. "It happens a lot."

"The same dream?" She nods. "About what?"

I can tell Monroe doesn't want to tell me the answer, but it's right on the tip of her tongue.

"Come on." I pull her back and she doesn't fight me, though her body is rigid with fear. "I'm not going to hurt you, Monroe. Just tell me. I'm here to help."

"I..." She bites her bottom lip, worrying it between her teeth. "I have nightmares about... something from my past."

Even though every word is hard to get out of her, I'm determined to find out the truth. I nod, saying, "I understand. A certain event from your past?"

"Yes."

"Who did it involve?"

She hesitates, nervously tugging on a strand of blond hair before finally muttering, "My stepfather."

"What happened?" She shakes her head, and now it seems like she's unable to get the words out. But I'm not going to give up that easily. One way or another, I'll find out the truth. "Tell me, Monroe. Please. I want to know."

"When I misbehaved..." Her voice cracks, but she clears her throat and forces herself to keep going. "He used to lock me in a closet when I was a kid."

"What the fuck?" My brows furrow, and my hands tighten into fists. Already, the need to beat the shit out of this prick is making me fucking pissed off. "Who does that? Why?"

She shrugs. "I guess he just thought it would make me more obedient."

"You were a kid," I growl. "How old were you?"

Another noncommittal shrug, and her eyes refusing to meet mine. But I'm not going to back town now, I'm determined to find out the truth.

"Tell me, Monroe."

"What's the point?" She manages a nervous smile. "All it will do is piss you off."

"Just say it."

"I don't know..." My determined glare makes her sigh before finally answering in a low whisper. "I don't know. Three or four, when it started."

"Are you fucking kidding me, Monroe?" I'm so pissed off I want to fucking kill someone right now. But since her stepfather isn't nearby, I settle for getting up and pacing the room, fighting the urge to smack my fist against the wall.

"Don't be upset," she mutters. "This is why I didn't want to tell you. Please. Don't be mad at me."

"I'm not fucking mad at you, Monroe." I run my hands through my hair, fighting my instincts to hunt down the bastard and kill him right the fuck now. "I'm mad at the prick who did this to you, and I'm mad I didn't find out sooner."

"There's nothing to be done now," she mutters. "It doesn't matter. And I'm over it."

I struggle with my reply, struggle showing her how I really feel. On the one hand, I know full well showing her my emotions will make me seem vulnerable and fucking weak, which I despise. But the urge to kill, to hurt, to maim, is making me fucking wild, and I don't know how to hold back for much longer.

"You shouldn't be over it," I balk at Monroe. "You should be seeking revenge for what the prick did to you. He should be in prison."

She shrugs. "It's better to let go than to dwell on the bad things others did to you."

I don't agree at all, but I can tell she still feels vulnerable and shaky, and my reaction to her confession is only making her close up more. So I rethink my anger, and get back in the bed beside her, once again pulling her against me and kissing the top of her head. "Go to sleep."

"What, with you here?" She narrows her eyes at me uncertainly. "Are you going to stay here?"

"Yes."

"But you... we... we don't do this."

"Tonight, we do." There's a determination in my voice that leaves no room for questions. The small smile playing on Monroe's face doesn't escape me as I pull her to me, and her body nestles into mine. She likes this. She feels safe.

"Thank you."

She says the words so softly I nearly miss them, but they register a second later. "What for?"

"For taking care of me," she mutters. "For giving me a job, taking care of me... It means a lot. I didn't know how messed up my life was, or maybe I was just living in denial. But this world you've introduced me to... It's so different. So new. I won't want to leave."

I'm tempted to tell her she shouldn't because I'm already getting attached and can't bear the thought of being without her. But instead, I say, "Good. Because you're not fucking allowed. You're a liability now, Monroe. I'm forced to keep you."

She turns around in my arms, obviously hurt by my words. I curse inwardly, hating myself for being such a prick. But it's how I'm wired, and it'll take longer than a few days to make me into something else. Already though, she's changing me into someone with fucking feelings, and I don't know if I like it. Feelings make you weak. And I don't *do* weak.

"Who's mad at whom now?" I mutter against her hair. "Come on, sugar. Look at me."

She shakes her head, but I've had enough. I put her on her back, climbing on top of her and holding her arms above her head. Her eyes glitter with the pain of my words as they meet mine, and I feel something I don't recognize tugging at my heart. Fuck. This girl will be the death of me.

"You don't have to act like keeping me is such a pain in the ass," she mutters, making me laugh out loud. She gives me an incredulous look. "What? You're acting like I'm a problem. Something you could be without."

I don't want to tell her the truth—that I want her by my side. That weakness I'm so afraid of is rearing its ugly head yet again, but I'm not going to let it win this time. "Stop sulking."

"I'm not sulking," she protests. "I'm just—"

But she doesn't get to finish her sentence. My lips cover hers, and I kiss her like I fucking own her, which I do. Our bodies mold together, crashing like waves and I claim her with every lick, every nip, every second our lips stay pressed together. I can tell Monroe wants to resist, but her body won't let her. She wants this, craves it. And I'm not going to stop. No matter how much she denies wanting me, the truth is written all over her pretty little face.

"You're telling me you don't want me sleeping next to you?" I ask her, trailing my tongue between her exposed tits. "You don't want my lips, my tongue, my fingers on you?"

"N-No." She struggles uselessly against me, but I'm not letting go. Holding her down firmly, I continue exploring her body. "Stop it, Alaric."

"I love the way you way my name," I grunt. "Fucking love it. Say it again."

"No." She struggles again, but this time, it's without any real effort. I smirk, knowing full well she doesn't really want to get away."

"Just stop."

"Stop?"

"Stop." She nods, but there's uncertainty in her eyes.

"Okay." I pull my arms away, watching her rub her wrists where I held on to them. "I'll leave if you want me to."

I make a move to pull back when she suddenly latches onto me. Her arms go around my neck, and she wraps her legs around my waist, making me unable to move. With a groan, I collapse back into the bed beside her, but she still doesn't move, clinging on to me for dear life. And the words she whispers into my ear fucking wreck me.

"Don't leave me," she whispers. "Everyone leaves me. Don't be like them."

I'm too deep in my thoughts to muster up a reply, so I just nod and hold her against my chest. In seconds, her breathing slows as she calms herself. It only takes a few minutes of stroking her hair and back for Monroe to fall asleep. This time, her breaths are slow and steady, and there's a smile on her face as she drifts to sleep.

No nightmares.

Not when I'm around, at least.

If only Monroe knew I'm what nightmares are fucking made of.

But I know it would scare her off. And I'm already getting attached. I can't risk losing her now, not when things are just starting to get good for us.

Holding her against me, I stroke her hair and don't sleep a wink. My thoughts are too full of the situation I got us in, too full of Monroe. She's got my head spinning, and I don't know if I like it or not.

But I don't have a choice, not anymore. I'm as far gone as she is, and only time will tell whether that's a good thing... or the beginning of the end.

10

MONROE

I don't know why I keep doing this to myself. I should know by now not to let anyone in, not to trust anyone. Every time I let someone close, they leave me. Every time I trust, I get disappointed. I should be used to it, and maybe I am, but it still hurts. The pain stays the same no matter how many people turn their backs on me.

Last night, I poured my heart out to Alaric. I told him my darkest secrets, which I haven't told anyone in a long time. I thought I felt something between us, some sort of connection. He held me when I needed comfort, and I was stupid enough to let him.

I let him hold me in his arms, cuddled into him like we are some kind of couple. I let him whisper sweet nothings in my ear while I cried myself to sleep, thinking this morning will be better. Things are going to change now.

I'm so naïve. Naïve and stupid.

That's all I can think of since I woke up alone and cuffed to the bed. Betrayal settles deep into my bones, and I keep telling myself

I need to hold on to this. I need to remember this, no matter how sweet he is at times. It's all lies, and he doesn't care about me.

I am his prisoner, his plaything, something he bought and put away when he doesn't need it at the moment. And when he's done playing, he's going to get rid of me. I have to get away before that happens because for Alaric, *getting rid of* means he's going to kill me.

The house is quiet, and I know he's not here because when I first woke up, I spent five minutes yelling his name. There's no clock in this room, so I have no way of telling the time, but my bladder tells me I need to get up and go to the bathroom.

I am so mad at him I entertain the thought of peeing in the bed out of spite, but I don't know how he would react, and frankly, I would be too embarrassed.

By the time I finally hear someone in the house, my bladder hurts from holding it for so long. I yell his name, and it doesn't take him long to appear in the room.

"Unless you want a yellow stain on your mattress, you need to hurry up and let me go to the bathroom."

"I didn't wanna wake you up, but I went to the grocery store and got some food," he explains but doesn't give me an apology. Not that his apology would mean anything to me.

He pulls the key from his pocket and quickly unlocks my handcuffs. I dash off the bed and into the bathroom, slamming the door shut behind me. Running to the toilet, I pull my panties down just in time to relieve myself.

Afterward, I take my sweet time in the bathroom, washing my hands and face, brushing my teeth, and combing my hair. It's a small act of defiance, but the thought of him waiting on me does make me feel a tiny bit better.

When I run out of things to do, I slowly open the bathroom door, ready to give him my best angry face, only to find he is not in the room anymore. I look around, dumbfounded, and even stick my head into the closet, but he is nowhere to be found.

Did he leave me here on my own... uncuffed?

The excitement of that thought doesn't even have time to build before I hear the sounds of dishes clinking together coming from the kitchen. So he didn't leave. Still, this is the first time he let me out of sight without restraining me. This is my chance.

I look around the room to find my clothes. Getting dressed quickly, I curse myself for wasting so much time in the bathroom. How long did he sit here and wait? When is he going to come and check on me? Maybe this is a bad idea.

Before I can talk myself out of this, I tiptoe to the window and unlock the two latches. I push it up... or at least I try to. Using both hands, I shove the window up using all my strength, but it won't budge. Confused, I scan the corners of the window and find a metal lock deadbolts to the edge. Fuck!

Briefly, I entertain the thought of trying to break the window, but I don't think I could, and even if I was able to, the loud sound would alert him before I could make it far. I need a better plan.

Balling my hands into fists, I take a deep breath, forcing the adrenaline from my failed escape to stop pumping through my body so he won't suspect anything.

When I find myself calm enough, I take off my shoes and put them back exactly the way I found them. I make my way into the kitchen and find him in front of the stove. The butter sizzles as he cracks eggs into a large pan, filling the space with a savory breakfast smell.

"I figured you would be hungry," he tells me. "I got eggs and bacon from the store, pancake mix too. I didn't know what you'd prefer."

"Yes, I'm hungry." I try to keep my voice even. "Eggs are great. I'm not picky." I've never had the luxury of being picky about food. When you grow up the way I did, either you eat what you have or you go hungry. Everything tastes good when you're hungry enough. "Can I help you with anything? I feel weird just standing here and watching you do all the work."

"You can get another pan for the bacon. It's in the cabinet under the kitchen island."

"Okay." I step past him to get to the island behind him. Leaning down, I open the cabinet and look inside. There are multiple frying pans and pots inside. I grab a skillet that's going to be great for bacon. I reach inside and wrap my fingers around the cast-iron handle.

As soon as I pick it up and realize how heavy this thing is, an idea forms in my head. Peeking over my shoulder, I make sure he is still turned away from me.

My eyes fall on his broad back, his muscles flexing beneath his shirt as he stirs the eggs. Gripping the handle tightly, I stand up straight and tiptoe behind him.

My heart is racing furiously, the rapid beat of it knocking the air from my lungs. I lift the heavy cast-iron pan over my head, cringing at the thought of hurting him. I've never hurt anyone, but I know I have to do this. I have to. For me and for Grams.

Squeezing my eyes shut, I swing the pan as hard as I can, aiming for the back of his head. The loud thud on impact vibrates through me, making my stomach twist with guilt. Alaric groans, and I open my eyes just in time to see his large body hit the ground. His head bounces off the tile floor, making me shudder.

Oh, my god! Blood trickles from the back of his head onto the floor, and suddenly, running away is the last thing on my mind. *Did I kill him?*

For a moment, I simply stand there frozen in place, still holding the pan because I don't know what else to do. More blood trickles from his wound, forming a small red puddle on the white floor.

What was I thinking?

"Ughh," Alaric groans, clearing the shock-induced fog from my mind.

He is alive. A mixture of relief and fear takes residence in my chest. He is alive, and he is probably going to kill me now. *I need to run!*

Squatting down next to him, I drop the pan and reach into his pants pocket. The moment my fingers touch the cool metal of the key, I grab it and pull it out. I run to the door and use the key to unlock it. It takes me three times before I can get it undone with my shaking hands, but the lock finally clicks.

I turn the knob and push the door open. Then I run.

Pushing my legs as fast as I can, I dash down the driveway and into the road. The houses are far apart, but the one to the right is the closest. Choosing that one, I sprint toward the front door, hoping, praying that someone is there who can help me.

"Monroe!" Alaric's gruff, angry voice echoes down the street, and my panic reaches new heights.

My muscles already ache, and my lungs are burning, but I still press harder, go faster. When I reach the neighbor's driveway, I hear Alaric behind me, his heavy footfall pounding against the pavement. He is closing in. He is going to get me.

"Monroe, do not knock on that door..." he warns, running after me. He is so close.

But I'm so close to the door. I can make it. I run up the five steps to the front door and start pounding against the heavy wood hysterically.

I get about three knocks in before Alaric grabs me from behind, his arms wrapping around me and pulling me back against his chest. I start struggling, immediately kicking out my legs and wailing my arms, but it's useless because he only holds me tighter. I'm just about to scream when I hear a woman's voice from the inside of the house.

"I'm coming." There is a cheerful tone to her voice, almost like she is expecting someone.

"Play along, or I will kill her," Alaric whispers into the shell of my ear, and my heart goes from hummingbird speed to zero. His threat isn't an idle one, and knowing that chills me to the bone.

Oh my god, what did I do? Not once did it cross my mind that I could put someone else in danger.

"Alaric, please don't hurt her," I beg for the woman's life I don't even know.

"Just play along."

Alaric shifts, draping his arm over my shoulder and standing next to me just when the door opens, and we come face-to-face with a middle-aged woman who's had a little too much Botox. She gives us a friendly smile, but there is a spark of confusion in her gaze.

"Good morning, Mrs. Henderson. I'm so sorry to bother you, but I'm afraid I left the door open last night, and my girlfriend's cat got out. I was wondering if you've seen it?" The lie falls off his lips so smoothly, I almost believe it myself.

"A cat? What does it look like?" She purses her red painted lips while staring straight at me, and I realize that it's supposed to be my cat.

"It's white with gray spots and black paw." I describe the cat I had when I was five.

"I'm sorry. I'm afraid I haven't seen a cat around, but I'll be sure to let you know if I do." Her eyes wander from my face down my body when they stop at my sock-covered feet.

"In my frenzy to get out to find my cat, I didn't have time for shoes," I explain. "I really love that cat."

"Uhm, okay." She looks at me dumbfounded.

"Thank you and sorry for bothering you again." I give her a tight smile, hoping she buys it. I've never been a good liar, but I've never had someone's life depend on it either.

Before she closes the door, Alaric has already spun us around, and we're heading back to his place. An apology sits on the tip of my tongue, but my throat is so tight I don't think I can get a single word out. Tears prick at my eyes, knowing that my life is probably about to end.

Alaric still has his arm around me, and if anyone sees us walking along the road, they probably think we're a couple taking a morning stroll. No one would ever know he is a hitman for the mob and I'm his captive. Nobody would suspect he is walking me to my execution.

When we get back to the house, he walks me inside and shuts the door behind us. I'm so scared my knees are about to give out. If he wasn't holding on to me, I would probably fall over. My vision is blurry from all the tears, and my throat hurts from my unspoken words.

"Why are you shaking? Are you cold or hurt?" Alaric turns me in his hold to inspect my face. "What's wrong?"

Is he fucking kidding?

He runs his hand over my arms and shoulders, almost like he is making sure I'm not injured. I'm so confused about everything, which is probably the reason I bury my face in his chest and wrap my arms around his torso, hugging him like he is my savior and not my executioner.

I fully expect him to push me away, to shove me to the ground or hit me. Instead, he wraps his arms around me and pulls me closer. I don't understand why he's doing it, but for the moment being, I simply let him hold me while I cry.

"I don't want to die," I tell him, my voice sounding just as shaky as I feel.

"I'm not going to kill you, Monroe. But if you try to run again, I will kill someone, and it will be your fault. You don't want that, do you? You don't want a death on your conscience."

"No, please. I won't run again." Releasing my hold on him, I put enough distance between us so I can look at him. Blinking my tears away, I study his face.

"Good. If you don't plan on running again, you have nothing to worry about. Now, go sit on the couch while I finish cooking breakfast."

"You're not going to kill me?"

"No. Though after we eat, I'm going to make you hold an ice pack to my head."

Not sure if he is joking or not, I do as I'm told and take a seat on the couch while Alaric finishes cooking us breakfast as if nothing happened. He cleans up the blood on the floor between flipping the bacon, and suddenly, I feel ashamed of what I did, no matter how justified it was.

Alaric brings me a plate, and we eat on the couch in silence. It isn't until I'm done with my food that the bottom of my foot aches. Lifting up my leg, I drape it over my knee to examine my foot. Blood has seeped through the sock right at my heel.

"Let me see." Alaric sets his plate on the coffee table and grabs my ankle. He pulls my leg into his lap and carefully slips off the sock to examine my heel. "I don't think anything is stuck in the wound. You probably just stepped on a rock. We'll clean it out and wrap it up. You should be fine."

"It didn't even hurt until now."

"Adrenaline numbs you up. If it hurts too bad, I can give you a painkiller." He cradles my foot like it's made of glass. My head spins with confusion. How can he be so sweet and caring one minute, and the next, he ties me to the bed while he goes off to kill people?

I don't think I will ever be able to figure him out. But one thing is clear—getting away is looking more and more bleak.

11

ALARIC

"This is really good," Monroe tells me between bites. She cuts another large piece of steak and dips it in the creamy pepper sauce. "But I have to say, I'm surprised you let me have the steak knife."

"I'm only worried about keeping heavy objects out of your reach." The back of my head throbs at the reminder, and guilt briefly flashes over her face, but it disappears just as quickly. I'm actually not mad at her for trying to get away. Truth be told, I'm impressed she managed to get as far as she did. I'm only mad at myself for letting it happen in the first place. I won't turn my back on her again.

"Trust me, little girl. I'm much faster and stronger than you. Not to mention, I was trained in hand-to-hand combat. It's more likely that you hurt yourself with that than hurt me."

She studies my face, and I can basically see the wheels turning. She is thinking about trying it, maybe even calling my bluff. I ready myself to fight off her attack, letting possible scenarios run through my mind. But then she simply shoves the steak into her mouth and chews slowly.

"Don't worry, I won't try anything...again. I would most likely only hurt myself."

My phone vibrates in my pocket, and I eagerly pull it out. Typing in the code, I unlock it and find the message I've been waiting for all day. It's from Dr. Houseman, letting me know that Monroe's test results all came back normal.

A rush of excitement fills my veins, to the point of not being able to sit still. Just thinking about what I have planned for tonight has my cock straining against my zipper. I shift in my seat. I'm not used to feeling this way, feeling so exhilarated about anything.

Monroe must notice my mood change as well. "Is everything all right?"

I clear my throat. "Yes. I just forgot the wine." Scooting my chair back, I get up and step into the kitchen. I stay on high alert while turning my back toward her. I won't let her sneak up on me again, but I am worried about her accidentally cutting herself.

While listening to her carefully, I get the bottle of chilled wine out of the fridge and pour two glasses. When I put the corkscrew back into the drawer, I slide my hand under the drawer inserts and grab the small clear bag with the tip of my finger.

Quickly, I open it and pour the contents into the wineglass. It dissolves right away, making it impossible for her to see. Dropping the empty bag into the sink, I grab the glasses and spin back around.

Monroe hasn't stopped eating and is almost done with everything on her plate. She was either very hungry or she really liked that food. No matter the reason, I'm glad she is eating. On an empty stomach, she would be more likely to get sick when she wakes up.

I hand her the glass of wine, and she takes it unsuspectingly. I watch her take a few sips while I sit down to finish my own food. By the time I'm done, Monroe has finished her wine, and I know it won't be long before she feels its effects.

"Monroe," I call her name, and her gaze lifts to mine. She tucks a strain of hair behind her ear, and I catch her hand trembling. She's smart and has good instincts. Her gut is telling her that this situation is off.

"Something is wrong," she states.

"I want to fuck you, Monroe," I admit. "But I have a certain way I want it to happen, a kink of mine I want to play out... I want you to be asleep."

Her eyebrows furrow together. She doesn't understand what I'm saying, or maybe she just doesn't want to.

"What do you mean...?" She trails off, the last word a little slurred.

I can see the exact moment she realizes what is going on. Her eyes go wide, and her lips part with an intake of a quick breath.

"You..." She can only get that one word out, but that's all she needs. That one word holds enough accusation, disappointment, and hatred for an entire speech. Regret trickles into my mind, but it's minuscule and quickly overwritten by the unbridled lust I'm feeling.

Monroe pushes up to her feet. The chair skates over the floor before falling over and hitting the tile floor with a loud crash. I get up just as quickly, knowing it won't be long before her legs give out.

I reach for her, but she frantically tries to get away, shoving against my chest. Her beautiful face is distorted with anguish, and I wish I hadn't told her anything yet. I should've waited a few more minutes.

"It's going to be okay," I assure her. "I won't hurt you, doll."

She sways to the side, suddenly reaching for me instead of pushing me away. I pull her closer as her knees give out, and she falls into my arms. I pick her up and carry her to the bedroom.

By the time I place her on the mattress, she's completely out of it. Her eyes are closed, and her hair falls into a blond halo around her head. She is so fucking beautiful. An angel I don't deserve... but I will have her anyway.

I undo my zipper and pull down my pants, needing to free my cock. It juts out like an iron pole. I don't think I've ever been this hard. This is my absolute fantasy, my deepest and darkest desire played out.

Yes, I've done this before, but it was different. The women I've done this with before knew what I was going to do. Monroe had no idea what was coming, and that part is a huge turn-on. But most importantly, the others weren't Monroe. They weren't as innocent and perfect as she is. No one measures up to her.

I strip out of the rest of my clothes until I'm completely bare. Then I start peeling Monroe's clothes from her sleeping form. I unwrap her like a present on Christmas morning. With every inch of skin I reveal, my excitement grows.

When she is completely naked, I grab the bottle of lube from the nightstand and pop the top open. I pour a healthy amount into my hand and put the bottle back. I coat my cock with it first, hissing at the cold liquid, then I use the remainder to rub it on her pussy.

I dipped my finger into her cunt, and it slides in with ease. She's tight, and she's going to feel so fucking good. I'm not small, and usually, I'd take longer to get her ready, but I can't wait another second without bursting at the seams. I've got to have her, and it needs to be now.

Positioning her sleeping form on the bed, I climb between her legs and line myself up with her opening. I wanted to go slow, I really did, but as soon as the head of my cock dips into her tight cunt, my brain shuts off.

With one hard thrust, I bury myself deep inside her warm channel. I never felt anything so good. It's like she was made for me. Her pussy grabs me, squeezing my dick so tightly it almost hurts.

I look down at her relaxed face and cradle her cheek as I fuck her gently for a moment. "My peaceful little angel. Sleeping while I fuck her cunt, while I dirty her up and make her mine."

Mine. The word runs through my mind on repeat.

Leaning down, I bury my face in the crook of her neck and start pounding into her without restraint.

It doesn't take me long to come with a roar. My balls tighten before emptying every last drop of cum into her waiting pussy.

Minutes pass before the haze of lust is lifted from my mind, and I'm able to think somewhat straight, but it isn't until I sit up to look at her that I realize something's wrong. My cock is coated in blood. More of it is smeared over her thighs and between her legs.

Fuck. What did I just do?

12

MONROE

I wake up oddly warm, a kind of warmth I haven't felt... well, ever. I try to blink my eyes open, but it feels like they are weighted, just like my limbs, which are hugged to my body tightly.

Trapped between sleep and wakefulness, I stay in limbo for what feels like a long time. Luckily, it's not such a bad place to be. I feel comfortable, content, and most surprisingly, safe.

My body and mind slowly come back to life. With each passing second, the fog surrounding my brain is getting thinner, and the feeling in my toes and fingers returns, letting me wiggle them awake.

When I'm able to move my arms again, I try to push the blanket tucked around me off, but it won't move an inch. As a matter of fact, it feels like it's only getting snugger.

"Shh... it's okay..." a deep voice rumbles close to my ear. It sounds like someone is whispering, but the sound is loud and vibrates through my body.

It takes me another few minutes to understand where I am and what is happening.

Dinner.

Alaric.

Drugs.

He fucking drugged me.

"It's okay," he repeats, and all I want to do is yell at him. It's not okay. Nothing is okay.

I force my eyes open, and they obey reluctantly. The room is dark. The only light illuminating some of the space is that coming from the cracked bathroom door.

Like a child, I'm swaddled into a blanket, two strong arms holding me in place against a firm chest.

As feeling returns to every part of my body, the dull ache between my legs becomes apparent. Oh god. He had sex with me while I was passed out. Tears sting my eyes as the realization of what he took from me sets in. He took my virginity while I was drugged and unresponsive.

A sense of loss hits me first, like he took part of me I will never get back. A part that I wasn't quite ready to give. On top of that, he robbed me of the experience. A rite of passage I will never go through now. I feel cheated and violated at the same time. It doesn't quite make sense. Shouldn't I be glad that I was passed out for this? Maybe this is the drug talking.

Anger washes over me next, like a tidal wave of fury, and I want to lash out, scream, kick, and break something, but all I can do is lie here.

My ear is pressed against his warm chest, which now explains why the whisper seemed so loud. The low thud of his heartbeat echoes in my head, and again, I feel oddly comforted when I partly know I should be anything but.

I'm being tugged in two directions. One is telling me to get away, and the other is urging me to get closer. The self-preservation part ends up winning the tug of war.

"Let go of me," I croak, barely recognizing my own voice. I squirm, hoping he would let me go, but his arms only tighten to the point of making it hard to breathe. "Stop!"

He loosens his hold, but only enough for me to tilt my head and look at his shadowed face. My anger reaches a new boiling point when I see him glaring down at me like I'm the one who did something wrong.

"Why didn't you tell me you were a virgin? I specifically asked you, and you lied to me."

"Are you making this my fault, you prick?"

His features soften a smidge. "I thought you were a..."

"A whore?" My voice is tinged with bitterness. "No. I don't do that stuff for money. I only did it for you."

"Why?" he demands.

"Because..." I chew at my bottom lip. "I don't know. The money."

"I'm sure others have offered you money, too. You like me. Admit it."

"No," I hiss. Hot tears spring to my eyes again, and I curse softly. "I can't even wipe my tears. I fucking hate you." And I do hate him, yet I rub my face against his bare chest, using him to soothe me.

"You should have been honest with me."

"Like that would have changed anything? Actually, maybe you would have done this sooner, knowing I'm clean."

Guilt flashes through his eyes so briefly I'm not sure it was there in the first place. "It doesn't matter anyway. It's done now." He keeps his head straight, staring into the dark corner of the room for a minute before he adds more quietly, "For what it's worth, I am sorry."

My first instinct is to tell him to fuck off. An apology is not good enough for something like this, but then I realize that apologizing is probably not something a man like Alaric does often, and somehow that fact makes his apology a little more potent.

That doesn't mean I forgive him. I don't think I can.

Alaric holds me for another few minutes without saying anything, and I'm almost falling back asleep even though I try not to.

"You need to drink something, or you're going to be dehydrated."

I roll my eyes at his words. Now he's worried about my well-being? I want to tell him no, but my mouth is, in fact, parched, and now that he's mentioned it, I can't stop thinking about anything else. He reaches over to the nightstand and grabs a glass of something.

Only when he brings the cold liquid to my lips and the tart lemon flavor hits my tongue do I know it's some kind of lemonade he is giving me. Greedily, I gulp the drink down until the glass is almost empty.

I feel a little better now but still weak. I don't think I could stand on my own right now. Settling back into his hold, I wait until the drug runs through my system.

"So this is your kink," I state.

"Yes, it is. Gets me hard fucking passed out girls," he tells me. His brutal honesty shouldn't shock me after what I know he's capable of, but it still does. He talks about it like it's the most normal thing in the world.

"Why?" I ask, genuinely curious.

"I don't know. Why is anyone the way they are? I've just always had this fantasy, and when I got older, I started playing it out."

"So I'm not the first one you've done this with?"

"No, you are not." I don't know why I care, but I do. Unwanted jealousy crawls up my spine, and I shove it away as much as I can. "Although the others were aware of what I was going to do. You were the first one I didn't tell before, which somehow added to the appeal. You made me so fucking hard, Monroe. I never came so hard in my life."

As fucked up as it is, pride blooms in my chest. I shove that into the same dark corner the jealousy ended up in and concentrate on how mad I am at him. "I'm sore… between my legs, I mean. It hurts."

"I'll give you some painkillers. I was definitely rougher than I should have been, but I didn't tear or bruise you. I checked. Of course I'm not a doctor, so if you want Dr. Houseman to come back, I can call him."

"No! I'm fine." The thought of him coming to give me another exam has my stomach in knots.

"All right then. Are you hungry?" At the mention of food, my stomach rumbles.

"Yes," I admit. No sense in lying. I need to regain my strength if I want to get away from him.

"I'll take you out to get something to eat. How does the diner on 6th Street sound?"

"You'll take me somewhere?" I ask, perking up. Excitement blooms in my chest, but a wall of doubt is standing between me and the outside. I'm not going to believe anything he says this easily.

"Did you think I'm going to keep you locked up in my house?"

"Yes," I tell him honestly.

"Well, I'm not, but you do have to follow certain rules while we are out." *Of course.* "You have to stay at my side the whole time. If you try to run, I'll chase you. Unless I'm in a bad mood and don't feel like chasing you, then I'll just shoot you."

"Great... why don't you just keep me drugged so I can't run."

"That's a good idea actually," he quips, calling my bluff. "Let me get it..." He moves me off his lap, and my heart leaps in my throat.

"No! I'll listen. I won't run," I promise.

A triumphant smile spreads across his lips, and I feel the urge to slap it off his face.

"Do you think you can get up, or do you need some more time? I'll help you either way."

"I'll try." I probably still need his help, and though I hate relying on him, knowing that he at least will help gives me comfort.

He unswaddles me from the blanket, and I push myself up to sit, which makes me realize I'm still completely naked. My first thought is to cover up, but that would be useless. He's already seen all of me... been inside me. The blanket falls away, and a shiver runs up my spine.

"I ordered you some new clothes. They were delivered earlier." He points at a box sitting on top of his dresser, and I swing my legs off the mattress. Eager to get to my clothes, I get up from the bed, but my legs are still too weak and give out as soon as I put my weight on them.

I brace for the pain when I inevitably hit the floor, but it never comes. Instead, a strong arm wraps around me, keeping me in place.

"Don't worry, I won't let you fall." His rough baritone in my ear calms down my erratic heartbeat. I hate that he has this effect on me. I hate that I lean into him, seeking comfort from the man who caused me to be this helpless in the first place.

He climbs off the bed while never letting me go. Supporting most of my weight, he walks me to the dresser so I can look into the box. As we move, I notice two things. One, he is wearing boxers. Two, he must have cleaned me up because there is nothing sticky or uncomfortable between my legs. I almost thank him for that, but then I remember how fucking ridiculous that would be. He doesn't deserve a thank you for that small sliver of kindness.

When we get to the box, I half expected to find skimpy dresses and high heels, but to my delight, I found comfortable-looking skinny jeans and soft, loose-fitting sweaters. Even the underwear he got is the same kind I would get, sexy but comfortable.

"How did you know what kind of stuff to get?" I ask while picking out an outfit.

"I went to your place, remember? I checked out your closet while I was there," he admits unapologetically.

"Right." *That's not creepy at all.* I would probably say that out loud if I wasn't so thankful for the clothes he got me.

Since I'm still so wobbly on my legs, he makes me sit down on the end of the mattress and helps me get dressed.

"What is it about the girl being passed out that turns you on?" I'm probably going to regret asking, but a part of me needs to know more, needs to make sense of this.

"I don't know. Why?"

"I'm just trying to understand you."

He finishes putting my underwear and socks on without a word. I step into the pair of jeans, and I'm convinced he's not going to answer me when he finally does. "I guess a part of it is her being helpless, unable to say anything. I'm in complete control. But then there is that other part, which might be even more appealing... there is no judgment. I can be who I am without pretending, without wondering what you might think of me."

"Oh..." I'm taken aback by the honesty in his voice. I feel like he just told me a secret he's never told anyone before. The question is, is that a secret I'm going to cherish, or is it really a nightmare I have to wake up from?

13

ALARIC

"Why don't I know anything about you?"

I raise my eyes to meet Monroe's. She's looking especially fucking delectable today in a pink floral dress and cute sandals that expose her pretty feet. The urge to bend her over the table consumes me, but I remind myself I need to behave in public. Still, all I want to do is bury my cock to the hilt inside all of her pretty pink holes. The thought is really fucking distracting, so I return my attention to my untouched plate of food in front of me.

We're sitting in the booth of the diner, having dinner. She's behaving for once, so I haven't been forced to handcuff her yet. But her question is probing, and I don't like it, so I growl, "Because that's how I like it. You don't need to know more than you already do."

"But I want to know more about you." She hungrily eats her waffles while I devour her with my gaze. Something about the girl is so damn enchanting. "I want to know where you come from and what your family was like. I want to know everything about you,

Alaric. What made you the person you are today. Tell me about your family. Please?"

"God, you're fucking stubborn." I pick at my omelet, my appetite waning. "My family... they're long gone by now. I told you already, I don't have a family anymore."

"But what happened to them?" she insists. Surprisingly, her stubbornness doesn't annoy me. It's kind of cute. "Why aren't they around anymore? Did you cut off contact? Did they? And why?"

"They're all dead, Monroe."

"Oh." She bites her bottom lip nervously. "I'm sorry, Alaric. I didn't even think... Did I upset you?"

"No." I shake my head, waving my hand dismissively. "It's in the past. I'm not hurting over it anymore. But I like to keep these things where they belong. Behind me."

"I understand. How... how did they die?" Her inquisitive eyes meet mine. She says she understands, yet her curiosity gets the best of her every time. "Your mom and dad."

"My dad died in prison," I find myself muttering. It's strange talking about this shit. It's been decades, after all, and I don't speak to anyone about my family. But something about Monroe's trusting gaze makes me want to open up for the very first time. "My mom... she was a drug addict since before my brother and I were born. When I was sixteen, she OD'd."

The silence hangs between us, heavy and charged with tension. Finally, Monroe reaches across the table for my hand, gently covering it with her palm as she whispers, "I'm sorry, Alaric."

"Don't be." I don't pull away, surprising myself. "She wasn't a good mother."

"And you said you had a brother?"

"Yeah."

"He's gone... too?" She looks so sad for me. But this isn't a sob story meant for her to feel sorry for me. It's a story of how I dragged myself out of the gutters and made a life, a name for myself. And I'm not going to feel bad about it. After all, everyone around me is long gone by now. And I'm the only one still breathing.

"Yes, he's gone."

"What happened?" she whispers.

"He died two years before my mom," I mutter. "He got shot in a drive-by. He was dead on the scene."

"I'm so sorry, Alaric."

"You don't have to keep saying that." I grin darkly. "I've made my peace with the past. I had to move on to save my own life. But I had help."

"What kind of help?"

"The Lombardis." It doesn't escape me how pale she gets when I mention that name. She's afraid of the Lombardis and for a good fucking reason. If I were handing out advice, I'd tell her to stay the fuck away from them. They're dangerous, lethal. But then again, so am I. "They gave me a home, took me in when my mom died. I had no one else. They took good care of me. But of course, they expected something in return. And that's how my training began."

"Your training... to be a killer?"

I don't get to answer Monroe's question because my phone rings. I scowl at the number displayed across the screen. "Sorry, sugar. I have to take this."

The call is quick and efficient, like always. It's a name, a location, and a date when it has to be completed. Except I don't even get a week or a day. It has to be done by midnight tonight.

My fist tightens around the burner phone as the call ends. I set it down and look warily at Monroe.

"What?" She knits her brows together in worry. "What is it?"

"There's something urgent I have to do," I mutter. "You'll have to come with me."

She pales, panicking. "But... you haven't even touched your food."

My food is the least of my worries right now. I'm more stressed about the fact that I'll have to drag Monroe to a kill site with me, and I didn't bring a pair of handcuffs.

"Come on." I toss a hundred-dollar bill on the table and motion for her to follow me. "We're leaving."

With trepidation, she falls into step beside me as we walk to my ride. On the drive over, she's quiet and pensive, and I can almost feel her quickened heartbeat without so much as touching her.

"When we get there, I'm going to have to lock you in the trunk of the car while I do my job."

"W-What?" Pure panic washes over her face. She's suddenly pale as fuck, trembling at the prospect of being locked up. And that's when I remember her past, what her stepdad did to her, how he locked her in a closet. Fuck. I don't want to do this, but I'm afraid I don't have a choice. "No, Alaric. Please. Don't do that to me."

"I don't have a choice," I grunt in return. "Especially with your attempt to run away. I'm not fucking risking it."

I pull up in a back alley while her panicked hands cling onto me. "Please. Don't do this to me. I'm begging you. Don't lock me in the trunk, Alaric, please, fucking please. I'm so scared."

I glance at her, trying to figure out another way to do this. But there is no other way. Either I lock her in the trunk, or she has to come with me. At this point, I'm not sure which option would mentally scar her more. They're both fucked up.

"Do you understand what I'm going to do in there, Monroe?" I hiss at her. "I'm going to hurt someone. And you'll be forced to watch."

"Please." Her panicked expression doesn't wane as she clings to me. "I swear, I'll be good. Just take me with you. Don't leave me here. I can't take it. I'll die."

I groan, cursing out loud. She doesn't leave me with much choice. The worst part is, I'm going fucking soft for her. I want to help her. I want to make her feel safe, but the option she wants is even worse than the trunk. She just doesn't know it yet. But then my sadistic side awakens. The one that wants to do this to her, wants to show her how I make the money that pays for her grandmother's nursing home.

"You want to come with me?" I ask to make sure, and her vigorous nod convinces me she does. "Fine. We're going in. Stick by my side, don't leave me for a second. Don't look at anyone. Don't make a scene."

"Yes, of course," she answers quickly. "Thank you, Alaric."

Her sweetness makes my heart hurt as it did before. It's an unwelcome feeling, especially since I've almost managed to convince myself I don't have a heart at all.

I get out of the car and open the door for her as well. We walk to the front of the building. It's a sleazy, shitty strip club I normally wouldn't step foot in. Purgatory is just so much better.

I grab Monroe's hand and drag her beside me. We walk into the joint, and I instantly feel everyone's eyes going to my pretty companion, devouring her. Anger simmers inside me, threatening to boil over as I drag her inside the club. She does as she was told and keeps her gaze trained to the floor. I want to tell her she's a good girl, but my tongue is tied. I need to focus on what I have to do here, what Monroe is about to witness. I need to step into the role of what the Lombardis made me—a murderer.

Someone approaches us, but I give the prick an icy glare. It's enough for him to back off. I know exactly what he wants—a taste of Monroe. But I'll sooner rip his fucking eyeballs out than let him lay a single dirty finger on my property. She's mine now, and I'm getting really fucking close to my breaking point. I almost want one of these shitheads to make a wrong move so I can punish them in front of my girl.

We walk into a VIP room, where my victim is. I push aside the veiled curtain blocking our entrance, already knowing what kind of scene we're going to walk in on. It's easiest to take the bastards down when they're balls deep inside a hooker. And that's exactly what's happening in the back room of this shitty club.

An old, balding man with a beer belly is fucking a strung-out looking girl, grabbing her dark hair as he grunts and drives himself deeper and deeper inside her cunt.

"What the hell?" Monroe whimpers. I don't let go of her hand.

"Get out," I bark at the dark-haired girl. She looks like she's about to argue, but then I flash her my red bracelet, and her eyes widen, making her look even more drugged up. My heart slows into a steady beat, and I'm in the zone, ready to fire a bullet at the old prick. He grunts as the girl moves away, and his semi-flaccid cock drops out of her pussy. The girl makes a desperate grab for some clothes, but I stop her, pulling out a gun. "I said get the fuck out. You don't have time for that. Fucking leave."

She lets out a soft shriek and runs out of the room stark naked.

"W-What the hell?" Monroe repeats, clutching my hand for dear life.

"You," I bark at the guy. "Your name David Hodge?"

"Depends who's asking," the prick slurs drunkenly. Finally, I let go of Monroe's hand, letting her tremble alone in the corner of the sleazy room. The guy is still naked as I walk him up to the wall and slam his back against it.

"I said," I continue icily. "Are you David fucking Hodge?"

"I-I-I..." He catches sight of my red bracelet, and his eyes widen with fear. "Please, man. Let's talk about this."

It's all the confirmation I need to know this is the prick I'm supposed to kill.

I pull out my gun while Monroe shrieks. Fuck, she's distracting. But I need to focus right now. I'll worry about my girl later.

I feed David the barrel of my gun, impassively watching his bleary eyes fill with tears.

"Look away, Monroe," I hiss.

"No!" she cries out. "Don't do this!"

"Look away!" My voice betrays how pissed off I am with her, and she whimpers as she looks down, softly crying as I pull off the safety of my gun. "Goodbye, David Hodge."

Unceremoniously, I paint the walls with the guy's brain. The gunshot rings out in the room, and David's lifeless body falls to the ground with a heavy thud.

It's over. It's done. And now, Monroe finally knows just how big of a monster I truly am.

14

MONROE

No, no, no! I can't believe this is happening again. Is this going to be my life now? Murder, blood, and mystery. How did I end up here? How did my life turn into this mess, and how do I get back to my normal, quiet life?

I stand there frozen in time, watching in complete and utter horror as Alaric takes a knife out of his boot and starts cutting off the guy's hand. The smell of blood permeates the air, making my stomach churn. But it's the sound of the bone cracking under the knife that has bile rising in my throat.

"Do not puke in here!" Alaric warns, "You don't want to leave evidence behind at a crime scene."

Slapping a hand over my mouth, I force myself not to throw up while wondering if I can make it. I don't think I can. What if I throw up? What if the police think I was involved in this murder? Oh my god. My mind reels, and thinking about all those possibilities just makes me more sick.

"Monroe! Look at me," Alaric orders. "You need to calm down. Everything is going to be fine, sugar. Just don't throw up, okay?"

"I'm trying," I say, still holding my hand in front of my mouth, making the words come out as a mumble.

I stare at Alaric as he finishes cutting off the dead guy's hand. I want to look away, but my eyes are glued to the gruesome scene that looks unreal. It's almost like I'm watching a movie, unable to control anything that's happening. It's like I'm an outsider looking in, but far away and safe.

Alaric wraps the severed hand up in a jacket hanging over a chair before tucking it under his arm like he is holding a rolled-up newspaper.

"Grab the bottle of vodka and pour it over my hands," Alaric tells me, pointing at a full bottle of Patrón at the table. I do as he asks and unscrew the bottle with shaking fingers. He holds out his hands to me, and I start to pour the clear liquid out until his hands are clean of blood.

"I have to bring this to my boss, and I don't have time to take you home, so you're going to have to come with me." I can tell by the way he's saying it that he is not happy about it.

Well, neither am I.

"How are we going to get out of here?"

"Walk." He shrugs. "Just act like nothing has happened. Maybe you should take a few sips of this before we head out." He nods toward the bottle of vodka remaining in my hand. Before I can think about it too long, I bring it to my mouth and take a healthy sip.

The alcohol goes down smoothly, only burning slightly at the back of my throat, and I embrace the warmth gathering in my stomach.

"Okay, I'm good... I think," I hiccup.

"All right, sugar." He wraps his arm around my back, tucking me to his side, and I try not to think about how he has a severed hand tucked under his other arm or that he is touching me with the same hands he used moments ago to kill someone.

Alaric opens the door we came from earlier. The music from the main floor gets louder, voices filtering through the hallways as he leads me through it and out the back. I say a silent prayer, hoping we don't run into anyone. I'm not good enough of an actress for this. I'm sure my horror is still all over my face.

I glance up at Alaric, but his face gives nothing away. It's like this doesn't affect him at all. He is neither scared nor shocked. Either that or he is simply good at hiding it.

He pushes open the back door, leading into the alley where we parked the car. Alaric walks me to the passenger side and helps me into the seat before shutting the door and walking around to get into the car himself.

The thought of making a run for it at that moment crosses my mind, but I shut that idea down quickly. I know he'd catch me in no time, and making him mad at me is probably not a good idea.

"You'll get used to it." Alaric breaks the silence after a while on the road.

"What if I don't want to get used to it?"

"We don't always get what we want. Sometimes we just have to go with it. I know you don't want this, but you are here now, and there is no going back. You've seen way too much, and I can't let you go... ever."

"Are you going to kill me?"

"Not unless you try to run. As long as you do as I say, I won't hurt you."

I nod and sink into the seat. I might be naïve to believe him, but somehow I do. For all the bad things I've seen him do, he's never hurt me physically, at least not on purpose.

"I have to drop this off at my boss's house, and I'm guessing you still don't want to be locked in the trunk?"

"No... can't I just sit in the car and wait for you?"

"No." He shakes his head. "I can't trust you not to make a run for it. Plus, in front of his house might be just as dangerous as inside."

God, I don't want to know what he means by that, and I don't ask. I look out the window and watch the large oak trees we're passing. I didn't even notice we had already left the city. The moon is large and bright, and the only thing shining light on the otherwise dark landscape.

After a few more minutes, Alaric turns into an unmarked dirt road, and my heart sinks. Did he lie? Is he driving me out here into the middle of nowhere to...

"Jesus, I can hear you think." Alaric chuckles. "My boss lives far out. He likes this secluded place. I already told you, as long as you listen, I won't have to hurt you."

A part of me still believes him, but doubt clings to me. I watched him murder a guy and cut off his hand less than an hour ago. But if he wanted me dead, he could have killed me there, right?

"Look, the house is coming up." Alaric points in front of him, and my eyes fall onto the large house in the distance.

The closer we get, the more I realize it's not a house at all. It's more like a mansion that could easily house eight large families. The driveway ends in a circle, the road wrapping around a fountain. I try to take everything in, but my brain is like a sponge full of water and can't hold anything else at the moment.

"Listen to me, Monroe." Alaric gets my attention, and I turn my head to look at him. "In there, you need to do exactly as I say. *Exactly*. Do you understand?"

My eyes go wide as I simply stare at him in shock. I want to tell him yes, but all I can do is look at him, wishing I was anywhere but here right now.

"Just like in the club, you keep your head down and stay close to me. Do not talk to anyone, don't look at anyone. Don't breathe toward anyone. You got it?"

Finally, I snap out of my fear-induced shock and nod my head furiously. "I'll stay glued to your side," I promise.

"Good." Alaric nods.

We both get out of the car and start walking toward the front door. I almost trip over my own two feet, but Alaric pulls me back up and tucks me to his side before I hit the ground.

Our feet touch the first step leading up to the entrance when the large double doors swing open, and two armed men pile out, guns raised. My knees lock, but Alaric pulls me farther up the stairs.

The two goons lower their guns, and I lower my eyes in return, remembering what I promised Alaric in the car.

"Sorry, you got here faster than we thought," one of the guys explains.

"Next time you point your gun at me, you better fire it, or it will be the last time you pull your gun at anyone," Alaric growls, letting his threat hang in the air as he marches us farther into the house.

I keep my eyes low, examining the marble flooring we're walking on, and only glancing to the side every once in a while when we pass a door. I don't see or hear anyone else until we get to the back of the house, and music carries into the hallway.

Alaric stops at the door the music seems to come from and reaches for the handle. As soon as he pushes it open, the music becomes loud, and multiple men's voices meet my ear.

"Alaric!" one of the men calls, and two more men chime in. "Good to see you, old friend. I'm guessing the job is done?"

"Alessandro, do I ever return without getting the job done?"

The group of men erupts into laughter. "Of course not, but just to ease my mind, you did bring what I asked you for, right?"

Alaric takes a few steps forward, and I follow him closely. I still haven't looked up at the men, but I can see the edge of a coffee table and a leather couch, both sitting on top of an expensive-looking carpet.

A thud sound has my eyes flicker to the table just in time to see the severed hand landing in the center. I gulp.

"Perfect. Now that business is out of the way, tell me about this fine little piece you brought to the party."

"This is Monroe, and I'm afraid we won't be able to stay and party with you this time. Maybe next."

A ripple of drunken complaints come from the men. I keep count in my head, and I'm pretty sure there are five or six guys total.

Alaric spins around, grabbing me by my arm a little rougher than necessary.

"Nonsense, Alaric. Stay, I insist," one of the men orders in a tone that doesn't leave room for an argument.

Alaric tightens his grip on my arm painfully, making me wince as he drags me to a couch. He sits down, then pulls me onto his lap. I keep my back straight, and my head down still, which only lets me see a little of the men sitting close to us.

"There you go. Here, have a drink," a different voice says. A moment later, a glass filled with ice and amber liquid appears in my view. Alaric grabs it while keeping his other hand planted on my hip.

"*Saluti*," all men say in unison, and I watch Alaric finish his drink in one gulp before slamming the glass on the table in front of us.

"So, Alaric," the man closest to us says. "Tell me, old friend. How much for her?"

All air whooshes from my lungs, and my whole body stiffens.

"She is not for sale, I'm afraid," Alaric answers calmly.

"Everything is for sale." The man laughs.

"Not her."

"You refuse to give me what I want, Alaric?" All the humor is gone from his voice now, and a deadly threat appears in its place. All the other men go silent as well, leaving the room to be eerily quiet. *What happened to the music?*

I try to breathe in, but my lungs won't work. My chest burns from the lack of air, and I know if I don't get this panic under control, I'm going to pass out soon. I close my eyes and concentrate on calming down when Alaric says something that makes me wonder if I've already passed out.

"You can't have her because she is my fiancée."

15

ALARIC

I don't know who is most shocked by the words that just came out of my mouth—me, him, or Monroe? She is sitting on my lap like she is frozen in time, completely still, every muscle tight.

Calling her my fiancée was the only thing I could think of, a split-second decision that will alter my entire life. I've never even thought about getting married before, but right now, this might be the only thing that will save her from Alessandro.

I owe this man my life. He is the only family I've ever known, but I know what he does to women. I know he likes to cause pain, and sometimes, he takes it too far and kills them. The thought of Monroe in his clutches makes my chest ache. Marrying Monroe might be drastic, but it's the only thing that will give her a chance to get out of here.

"So you want Monroe to join this family?" Alessandro asks, eyebrow raised. When I nod, he continues. "You know what that means, right? She needs to prove her loyalty to us."

Fuck. I didn't think that far ahead.

"She has to go through initiation just like anyone else. She will have to kill someone for the family."

Monroe's head snaps up at his words, all blood drained from her face as she looks at me with impossibly wide eyes.

"I guess I should introduce myself first if you are going to be part of this family. I'm Alessandro Lombardi. This is my younger brother, Savio, and some of our close friends," he introduces everyone one by one before turning back to Monroe. "So, who are we going to have you kill for us?"

Monroe's mouth falls open like she is about to say something, but no words come out.

"Don't be ridiculous, Alessandro," Savio interjects. "She doesn't have it in her to kill someone, and you know it. There are other ways she can prove herself. We can plant her for information or use her as bait. Those would be much smarter choices since she has no affiliation with us until now. No one would suspect her."

"Maybe smarter, but certainly less fun." Alessandro leans back in his seat, running his hand over his chin in thought. "However, I can think of something she could do for us, something that would prove her loyalty to this family, and the best part, it can be done today."

The mischievous glint in his eyes tells me I don't want to know what he has in mind. Nevertheless, I ask, "And what would that be?"

"Fuck her in front of us and give us a show." He smiles. "If you won't let us fuck her, that's the least you can do." The other guys in the room nod their head in agreement, their eyes already undressing Monroe like the hungry hyenas they are.

"Those are your choices. Either she kills someone, we get to fuck her, or you fuck her in front of us."

Monroe is shaking on my hold as I take a moment to weigh my options. There is really only one choice that would keep her permanently unharmed. "Fine, I'll fuck her, but no one else touches her. She is mine."

Alessandro holds up his hands and chuckles, "I get it, she is your new toy, and you don't like to share... yet."

Ever. I won't share her ever.

"Pour me another one," I hold out my glass, and Savio pour another inch and a half of bourbon into my glass tumbler. Instead of drinking it myself, I bring the rim to Monroe's trembling lip. "Drink."

She takes a small sip, wrinkling her nose at the taste, but then downs the entire contents with her second gulp.

"Stand up," I order softly, pushing gently on her back.

She stands up like a newborn fawn. Her steps, I'm sure, are shaky. I keep my hand planted on her lower back and lead her to the couch on the other side of the room.

She flinches when I reach for the hem of her shirt, and I have to grind my teeth together to stop myself from reassuring her that everything's gonna be okay. She lifts her arms, and I pull the shirt over her head, exposing most of her smooth, unblemished skin.

I reach for her bra next, unclasping the back. I let it fall off her shoulders and onto the floor. She immediately lifts her arms to cover herself up, but I shake my head and pull them down. Obediently, she lets her arms fall next to her and lets the men gawk at her like she's nothing more than a piece of meat.

"That's a nice pair of tits... fuck, I wouldn't mind sucking on them..." Bruno, one of Alessandro's goons, groans. The others chime in, and I have to force myself to keep going.

Ignoring the men's catcalling and crude comments, I reach for the button on her jeans and start undoing them. Even with all the men watching, I can't help getting hard myself when I pull down her jeans to expose her barely covered pussy. Her white cotton underwear is so thin I can see the outline of it, and knowing how tight she is has all the blood rushing to my cock.

But before I sink deep into her cunt, I need to make sure she's good and ready.

Dipping my fingers into the waistband of her panties, I pull them down her smooth legs, exposing her clean-shaven pussy, which immediately gets ten comments from the other men.

I want to growl *mine* like a rabid dog so they will all know to stay away from her. Instead, I grab her hips and bury my face in her pussy. Running my tongue through her slit, I make her whole body shudder with the intrusion. Her hands come to my shoulders, and her nails dig into my skin through the shirt I'm wearing.

Her feminine musky taste hits my tongue, driving me even more insane, but having my back to Alessandro is not sitting well with me. Giving her one final lick, I pull my face away and gently push her back to sit on the couch.

"Spread your legs for me, sugar," I tell her, imagining we are the only two people in this room. Her eyes stay glued on mine as she obeys and spreads her legs so everyone in the room can see her pink little pussy and spread out asshole.

"Suck," I order, bringing my middle finger to her mouth. She wraps her plump lips around my finger and around her tongue over it as she sucks on it like she's been told.

When my finger is good and wet, I pull it out and bring it between her thighs. She gulps, clearly nervous but doesn't say a word when I slowly push the single digit into her welcoming heat.

Monroe stays completely still as I finger fuck her gently at first. But when I add my thumb to her clit, she starts wiggling around and grabbing onto the pillows beside her. I pick up speed and increase the pressure on the small bundle of nerves, but it isn't until I add a second finger that her thighs start quivering, and I know she's about to come.

I can tell she's holding back, trying not to come, which only makes me want to make her come more. I hate that everyone is watching, but even now, I want her to come apart by my touch. I want to control her body, control her pleasure.

It only takes another minute before her head falls back and her whole body tightens. Her pussy squeezes my finger, and a muffled moan falls from her lips. I drown out the hollering from the other men in the room and concentrate on her and only her because right now, that's the only way I'm going to be able to go through with this.

16

MONROE

This has to be a nightmare. A bad dream I'm going to wake up from any minute now. None of this is real. Alaric did not tell me he was going to marry me, and he definitely didn't just make me come while his friends were watching.

Squeezing my eyes shut, I say a silent prayer to the universe, asking to wake the hell up from this, but when I blink my eyes open, I'm still here. Still in a room full of men who have their dicks out.

They are all watching me, their lustful eyes glued to my naked body as they stroke themselves. Two of them even have their phones out filming me. Fucking Christ. I've never felt so ashamed in my life. My legs are still spread, giving them a perfect view of the most private part of me.

"Look at me, not them," Alaric growls, and my attention snaps back to him. My eyes lock with his, and my breath stills in my lungs. His eyes are so dark they are black. He is looking at me with such intensity my body starts shaking again.

He is removing his clothes, exposing his taut muscular body like he is flexing every muscle at once. He seems bigger, more dangerous, almost feral. At that moment, I don't even care who is watching. I just care about him not shredding me to pieces.

When he is completely naked, he wraps his hand around his hard cock. My eyes travel down to the iron rod between his legs, and my mouth goes dry. I know he's been inside me before, but I was not conscious then, and the day after, I was sore as fuck. I can't imagine this will bring me anything besides immense pain.

Foolishly, I try to close my thighs, but Alaric is faster. Shaking his head, he positions himself between my legs, grabbing my knee to keep me spread.

"You're going to keep your legs spread until I allow you to close them. Do you understand?"

"Yes." I nod. Right now, I'm so scared I'd agree to anything he said.

"Fuck yeah..." The men start egging him on, yelling vile things at him. "Fuck her ass, make her bleed..." I try to tune them out, but their voices echo around in my head, taunting me, Their words reaching me where their touch never could, staining my soul.

Alaric moves closer until his cock is inches away from my pussy. He leans forward and rubs the angry-looking head of his dick over my still sensitive folds. I wince at the contact. Not because it hurts but because I'm already scared it will.

"You gonna take my big cock up your tight cunt, and you're not going to fight me, got it?" Alaric warns, the possessiveness in his voice shocking me. "You're going to be a good girl and take whatever I give you."

I nod, unable to get a single word out at the moment. The lump in my throat feels like it's never going to get dislodged, and I wonder if I'll be able to say anything for the rest of the night.

Without warning, Alaric pushes forward, entering me slowly but forcefully. Pain shoots through me, and I bite the inside of my cheek, keeping my mouth closed to muffle a scream as he shoves his too-big cock into my tight channel. I feel like he is ripping me apart, tearing open my insides while I lie back and do nothing.

Tears prick at my eyes, and even though I try my best to hold them back, they fall down my cheeks anyway.

"God, you are so fucking tight," Alaric grunts while filling me to the max. When he is all the way seated inside me, he holds still for a few seconds before slowly pulling out again. The next time he thrusts inside, it's faster and more brutal, but the pain stays the same.

The other men in the room are still talking, but I'm finally able to drown them out, their voices nothing more than an inaudible murmur. Instead, I hear Alaric's grunting and my heavy breathing while he continues to fuck me at a furious pace.

Squeezing my eyes shut, I wish for this to be over soon, for Alaric to take me home and hold me until I go to sleep. That thought evaporates when he shifts on top of me. Grabbing my hips, he grinds his pelvis over my clit, and a spark of pleasure reignites.

Only then do I notice that the pain is almost gone, leaving me feeling mostly full and uncomfortable everywhere. Well, everywhere but my clit, where his grinding has a different kind of pressure break out. Suddenly, I feel hot all over, like my skin is burning up, and I think I could actually come again.

How is this possible? How can he make me feel this way in front of all these men? I'm so ashamed of myself. I didn't ask to have sex in front of them, that part is out of my control, but to orgasm? That's on me. I should be able to control that. I shouldn't want him to keep touching my clit until I come, but right now, that's exactly what I want.

I'm almost there, right at the cliff, about to go over, when Alaric pulls out of me abruptly, making me wince at the loss. My eyes fly open, just in time to see a knowing smirk on his face.

"Turn around, sugar," he orders, but before I can move a muscle, he flips me around himself, propping me up until I'm folded over the back of the couch and facing away from him and all the other men.

I'm on my knees, my ass up in the air, and my legs slightly spread. I can feel Alaric moving behind me, his large hands roaming over my ass and thighs until he grabs both of my ass cheeks and spreads them apart.

My face feels like it catches on fire, and I'm glad that I can at least not see the men looking at me. Lowering my head, I rest my cheek on the back of the leather couch while Alaric runs the tip of his dick up and down my slit, then even further over my puckered asshole.

I clamp up right away, squeezing my ass cheeks together and making everyone in the room break out into laughter. Anger replaces my shame and fear momentarily. How dare they laugh at me? Fucking pricks. I dig my fingers into the plush leather where I'm holding the edge of the couch, imagining my nails would be digging into their eyes instead.

Alaric leans close, keeping his voice low so only I can hear the whisper, "Not today, little one, but soon... soon, this ass is going to be mine. Every part of you is mine. Don't you ever forget it."

A shiver runs up my spine at the same moment Alaric thrusts forward, entering me in one swift move from behind. My pussy quivers around his cock, this new position hitting a spot deep inside me I didn't know existed.

This time, I can't stop the moan from slipping past my lips. Fuck, this feels good. There is still a little bit of pain, but that's pushed in the background while pleasure consumes me.

Alaric keeps fucking me like a man possessed. Holding my hips with a bruising grip, he pounds into me so hard the couch scoots across the pristine marble floor slightly. Pleasure keeps building inside my core until it finally erupts.

I held the orgasm as long as I could, which might be the reason I come so hard my vision goes black for a moment. My body slumps against the couch like I'm boneless. My cheek rubs against the leather as Alaric's thrusts become erratic.

I'm still coming down from my own release when Alaric stills deep inside me with a grunt, his fingers digging into my hips painfully as he fills me with his warm release.

I feel drained, defeated, but also oddly sated. With Alaric still inside me, his heavy body leaning on me, I feel protected, shielded from everyone else. When he pulls out, I can feel his cum run down the inside of my thigh, and shame slams back into me with a vengeance.

The fog of lust is lifted, and the voices of the other men in the room become clear again.

"Look at that cum running out of her cunt... You fucked her good. Maybe you can fuck my wife for me like that... Are you sure you don't want to fuck her ass? I wouldn't mind seeing her asshole gaping..." Their crude words make me want to curl into a fetal position and cry my heart out.

I can feel Alaric moving behind me, but I don't turn around to see what he's doing. Not until he throws something on top of my body. I look over my shoulder and find him fully dressed, wrapping me up in what I now realize is a blanket.

He tucks the soft fabric around me tightly, then picks me up and cradles me to his chest.

"I'll see you soon, old friend," Alessandro tells him before settling his dark gaze on me. "And you as well, Monroe."

Without answering, I turn my head away and bury my face into Alaric's chest as he starts walking us out of the room and through the mansion. I keep my eyes closed and my face hidden, letting Alaric's spicy cologne calm my nerves until we make it outside, and his scent is replaced with the crisp fresh air of nature.

Alaric somehow manages to open the passenger door without putting me down, then carefully deposits me in the seat and buckles me up. He doesn't say a word as he closes the door and walks around to get into the driver's seat.

Silently, he starts the car, and we drive back to his place, leaving the mansion and everything that has happened there behind in the darkness. My only fear is that it won't stay there for long.

17

ALARIC

I've done a lot of fucked-up shit in my lifetime, but this has to be the biggest mess I've gotten myself into so far.

I watch Monroe sleeping. She looks like an angel, so innocent, so pure. Her blond strands of hair cover the pillow, and her full lips are slightly parted. Her heavy chest rises and falls as she sleeps, and my cock hardens at the sight. Fuck, I can't help myself around her.

What the hell was I thinking last night? I should never have introduced Monroe as my fiancée. Now I'm fucked. I have to marry her or risk the Lombardi family getting their dirty hands on my girl.

Still, I don't regret it. I can't bear the thought of Alessandro getting his hands on her. I'd have to kill him for it, and then I'd really be in a world of trouble.

Before my eyes, Monroe yawns and stretches in the bed like an innocent kitten.

"Good morning," I grunt.

"Morning." She rubs her eyes and looks up at me. Her expression is so trusting it fucking hurts. She shouldn't trust me. I'm a fucking monster. Yet I can't help myself, even though I know it would be best for Monroe to hide her away somewhere where the Lombardis won't find her.

I watch the memory of what happened last night dawn on Monroe, and her expression darkens as she remembers everything I put her through yesterday. Her bottom lip trembles, making me feel guilty as fuck.

"What's going to happen now, Alaric?" she asks softly.

"What has to happen," I reply firmly. "Tomorrow, we're going to get married. Today, we're going to look for a wedding dress."

Monroe's jaw hangs open as she realizes I'm totally serious. But I don't leave her any room to argue. I usher her into the bathroom and take my sweet time washing her myself. As my strong arms roam her gorgeous, voluptuous body, I find it hard not to fuck her then and there. But I resist the urge. Instead, I soap her up and lather her hair with shampoo.

"Why are you being so caring?" she asks softly.

"Someone has to take care of you," I mutter in response, washing the suds off her full tits.

"I can take care of myself, thank you very much."

I smirk at her, saying, "You aren't resisting much for someone who's so determined to be independent."

She flushes, not arguing anymore as I wash the shampoo out of her hair. Once we're done, I wrap her up in a towel and watch her intensely as she dries her hair, styles it, and puts on a small amount of makeup. She looks so fucking stunning it hurts. The only thing that hurts more than her beauty is the thought of some prick getting his dirty hands on her. And this only strengthens my resolve to make Monroe mine once and for all. I can't risk Alessandro stealing her, and the only way to prevent that is to marry the girl.

I take her to an upscale wedding boutique where an overly friendly employee happily chatters to Monroe as she guides her between the rows of hangers. I see my girl checking the price of one of the dresses discreetly. She pales. The dress probably costs more than a year of care in her grandmother's nursing home.

But she's worth it.

"I must say, it's quite unusual for the groom to come dress shopping with the bride!" The sales attendant is smiling at me widely, and I fight the urge to snap back. "But whatever works for you two lovebirds!"

I mutter something incomprehensible in response, my eyes still following Monroe as she moves through the shop.

"I'm going to take the bride to the back to try something on now," the attendant beams, but when she tries to walk away, I block her path.

"No," I hiss, making her swallow thickly as her heavily made-up face falls. "I don't want you alone together. I want to watch her change."

"Oh?" The lady chuckles nervously. "I must say, that's very unusual..."

"I don't care," I bark. "I'm paying you enough so you don't ask stupid questions. Either I watch her change or she's not trying anything on at all."

"Of course." She smiles, obviously freaking out. She probably doesn't know shit, so even flashing my red bracelet won't work. But she's too afraid to argue with me, even though she's uncomfortable as fuck.

"Which one do you like?" I ask Monroe a moment later.

"Does it matter?" she whispers, earning another curious look from the saleslady. "It's not like this is my dream wedding. So who cares?"

"Just pick something," I hiss while my bride-to-be sighs and keeps browsing the racks.

Finally, she pulls out a few dresses, and the overly enthusiastic sales lady takes them all to the changing room. I follow the two women there, taking a seat on a plush beige armchair. I force Monroe to keep the curtain in the shop open. I slipped enough money in the saleslady's pocket to ensure we're the only ones in here, and I've seen her naked already. While the assistant, a prim-and-proper girl in her late twenties, fills my glass with champagne, my eyes are glued to Monroe slipping off her clothes while her cheeks burn with shame.

She must be hating this, and I really must be a fucking prick because I'm loving winding her up.

Monroe tries on the first dress. It's a frilly thing with so many ruffles I can barely make out her body underneath the layers of fabric.

"No," I bark the moment she comes out in the fabric.

"What do you mean, no?" Monroe whines, turning to the side. "I love it. I look like a princess."

"Next," I mutter, checking my phone. "Try something more revealing."

She rolls her eyes and walks back into the changing room.

"You two are so cute," the assistant gushes, and I give her a doubtful look.

"How about this one?"

Monroe reappears, this time in a tight satin gown with a train. It clings to her body, exposing everything I love about it.

"Better," I mutter even though I love the dress. But I'm not going to tell her how stunning she looks in front of these two nosy women. I'm saving that for when we're alone in bed, and Monroe's riding my dick to an orgasm.

I nod at the saleslady, saying, "We'll take it."

"Well, that was fast!" She looks delighted as I pay in cash for the dress. She doesn't even bat an eye at the stack of hundred dollar bills I hand over to her. "We'll need to make some alterations of course, so it fits your bride perfectly."

"That's fine. Just make sure it's fast." I scribble an address on a piece of paper. "When it's done, send it here."

"Of course, sir."

I march Monroe out of the store, feeling her eyes on me. She wants to ask something, I can tell. And finally, she lets herself spit it out.

"What was the address you wrote down?"

I was worried about this question and even more worried about telling her the answer. But she doesn't really have a choice. I'm going to decide for her.

"It's Alessandro's house," I tell her firmly, without any room for further questions. "That's where we're getting married."

Monroe stops in her tracks, her brows knitting together. "I don't want to get married there. I don't like the guy."

"The feeling is mutual, sugar," I say. "But you don't have a choice, and neither do I. We need to convince him we're in love or he won't stop trying to get his hands on you. And we don't want that, do we?"

"No," she says softly. "But I still don't like it."

"I know." I squeeze her hand. "But it's going to be okay, I promise. Now come on."

I open the car door for her, and she gets in. I follow on the driver's side and start the car while she pensively stares ahead, refusing to talk. I let her stew in her anger. There's not much I can do to make her feel better, so I think it's best if I just let Monroe work through it herself.

"What about the money?" Monroe suddenly asks, making me look at her out of the corner of my eye as we drive.

"What about it?"

"Are you... are you going to honor the deal you made with me?"

"Monroe," I say. "You don't need to worry about money anymore."

I can tell there's another question on the tip of her tongue, but before she can express her concerns, I speak up again.

"Your grandmother is taken care of."

"W-What?" Her eyes are panicked as they meet mine again. "How... how did you know?"

"I did a background check on you, obviously." I stop the car in the parking lot of a mall so we can speak without worrying about the road. "I had to. I needed to know you weren't a liar."

"Please." She looks panicked now, a look of pure fear taking over her pretty face. "Please, don't hurt my grandmother. She's everything I have. Please, Alaric. Promise me she won't get hurt. Not because of me."

"Don't worry." I take her chin in my hands and gently tip it back so she's forced to look at me. "I won't let anyone hurt her. There's no reason anyone should find her, either. I'm paying for her care from an off-shore account. She's safe."

Monroe nods, but her bottom lip is trembling as she looks up at me. "I just... I can't bear the thought of Gram getting hurt because of me. I'd never be able to forgive myself."

"I understand." While I don't have a relationship with family, I do get her. She wants to keep the innocent party in all this safe, and since I'm her future husband, it's now my job to take care of her loved ones. "Like I said, nobody will find out, and she'll be safe. Don't worry. I promise you, nothing bad will happen."

She nods, and from the trusting look in her eyes, I can tell she believes me, which makes me grin.

"How often do you usually see your grandmother?" I ask next.

"I try to go twice a week," she responds. "Although sometimes I can only manage it once a week. Depends on my shifts."

"So it's been a while. You think she's worried?"

"She must be." Monroe nervously twists her arms in her lap. "I call her every day. She's surely wondering why I haven't been in touch."

A pang of guilt hits me hard, shocking me. I don't do guilt. I don't have a conscience. And here I am worrying about some old lady I have no connection to.

"We could go see her." The impulsive words shock me as much as they do Monroe.

"Me and you?" She laughs softly. "I don't think so, Alaric."

I shrug, turning the car back on. "Suit yourself. But the only way you'll see her is with me in tow. If you don't want to, though, it's fine. Just thought I'd offer."

Out of the corner of my eye, I can see her trying to decide what to do. She chews her bottom lip, nervously glancing at me as I continue to drive.

"Visiting hours are over by now, anyway," she mutters. "It's too late to go there."

I smirk, turning the car around, already knowing I've got exactly what I wanted. And I guess I'm about to meet my fiancée's grandmother. I can only hope she accepts me and doesn't cause a scene. But something tells me Monroe's grandmother is somewhat like her granddaughter, and I'm going to like her.

Monroe stares at me as I wink and start driving to the nursing home, the address for which I looked up a few days ago.

"You know I like to break all the rules, sugar."

18

ALARIC

Monroe is quiet for the rest of the drive to her grandmother's nursing home. I can tell she's nervous about me meeting her only relative, and I understand why. She's seen me do some fucked-up shit, and now she has to introduce me to the person who means most to her in the world. It might be a shit show... so I need to be on my best behavior.

We pull up in the posh driveway of the home. It's on a large piece of land with a large stone mansion covered in ivy. The grounds are well-maintained, and the seniors walking around are wearing big, pleased smiles. As Monroe and I get out of the car, one of their smiles grows bigger and bigger.

"Monroe!" An old lady waves us over enthusiastically. She's sitting by a pond with a friend who's already wheeling away. "Over here, honey!"

Monroe flies forward while I inspect her grandmother. The woman has a calm, quiet confidence to her I like. She seems like the quintessential grandmother I never had. The kind that may be vulnerable in body, but is a force to be reckoned with in any other way. I decide I like her on the spot.

Watching as Monroe hugs her tightly, I grin at the woman. "Hello, Mrs. Smythe. My name is Alaric."

"Alaric?" She nods, kissing her granddaughter's cheek and clinging to her hand as Monroe pulls away. "What an unusual name, and such an unusual man, too. You know, you're the first one she's brought over to see me."

"Gram!" Monroe flushes deeply, and I smirk, reveling in the fact that she didn't bring me over. I forced myself into Monroe's life, after all. And she fucking loves it.

"I expect nothing less of her. She's very picky," I smirk. "It took me quite a while to convince her I was a stand-up guy. Well... sometimes I wonder if I still haven't *quite* convinced her."

Mrs. Smythe laughs. "I know just how stubborn she can be. I did look after her until she was three years old."

I nod, ignoring Monroe's death glare in my direction. She wants me to stop asking all these prying questions and playing a game, but we have to, for her grandma's sake. I don't want to know how she'd react if she knew the truth...

"Gram, is everything going well here? They taking good care of you?" Monroe interrupts.

"For the most part." Her grandmother smiles. "There is one lady who I think is stealing my socks."

"Oh." I can tell Monroe is holding back a giggle. "Which one is it? I'll talk to her."

"The one with the pretty purple hair." Mrs. Smythe nods toward the entrance of the building where two nurses are watching the seniors. "Her name is Faye."

Monroe rushes in the direction of the nurse while her grandma turns to face me with a smug smile.

"Stealing socks, huh?" I tease her.

She winks and pulls up the leg of her trousers to reveal a pair of striped pink and white socks. "Count all my pairs every night. Not one missing so far."

"Sneaky." I chuckle. "You wanted to talk to me alone."

"Of course." She smiles back. "I need to find out if you're worthy of my granddaughter."

"Well, fire away," I respond. "Ask me anything you want."

"Well, all right. Say," she goes on, eyes glittering with mischief. "I couldn't help but notice... is that a red bracelet around your wrist?"

Sharply, my eyes find hers. "Indeed it is."

I can't say more than that. Can't risk her asking more questions—but this one alone has me sweating. How could she know the significance of the red ribbon tied around my wrist? Unless... unless *she's part of it, too.*

"Well, first of all, I think you should call me Ida." She grins before shakily pulling back her sleeve to reveal a green ribbon tied around it. "They make me wear it, even now."

I pale. "You work... for the Lombardis?"

"I did once upon a time." She nods gravely. "I helped with their accounting. I had to serve a sentence when Monroe was a toddler. That's why she was stuck with that awful stepfather of hers."

"I have heard some horrible stuff," I mutter. "I couldn't imagine why she wasn't living with you."

Ida nods. "I only got back a few years ago, and now I live here. And I know how much Monroe is paying for me to stay here, and I feel truly guilty."

I reach for her hand, trembling on the blanket covering her legs. "Don't, Ida. She loves you. And I'm helping her out now. She won't want for anything."

"No, she won't," she says somewhat sharply, sighing before she pulls her hand away from mine with surprising strength. "I tried my whole life to protect Monroe from that family. And now you've walked in, and you work for them, too. How am I supposed to believe Monroe won't be in danger because of you? She's been through so much."

"I would never let her get tangled up with them." I pull back but keep my eyes on Ida's. "Believe me. I'm doing all this to keep her safe."

"All this?" She narrows her eyes at me. "So you don't love her."

"I..."

"Are you marrying her?" she demands.

"Y-Yes, that's what we came to tell you," I manage to get out.

"Then you should love her. And I will not speak to you until you admit it to me." She raises her head high in the air and wheels away from me. I'm left stunned, but I still rush after her, getting in front of her wheelchair and stopping her.

"Ida—"

"Mrs. Smythe," she interrupts.

"No, no, you can't go back on that." I grin, and a reluctant smile pulls on the corner of her lips. "Ida it is. And look. Your granddaughter... she means a lot to me. Which is not an easy thing for me to say. You've seen the ribbon, and you know what it means, don't you?"

"Yes." She nods gravely. "The green one is for people who don't spill blood. The red one is for the ones who do."

"Then you know why mine is red, and what I've done to earn it. And I understand why you're afraid. But Ida, I won't let your granddaughter get caught up in it."

"Seems to me like you already have," she mutters, still not entirely happy with what I'm saying. "It's inevitable. And in this town, it was going to happen sooner rather than later."

"I will keep her safe," I insist. "And... with the way my feelings are developing, I may not be too far off from what you want."

Now, her eyes finally start to sparkle, just as Monroe returns.

"She said she wouldn't steal any more socks," she tells her grandmother with a triumphant smile. "And she said she's very, very sorry."

"Good. Now, when is the happy day?"

"You told her?" Monroe balks at me. "You were... you weren't supposed to do that!"

"I may be too old to be at your wedding, but I'm glad I know about it." The older lady smiles. "I hope you have a beautiful life together, Monroe. I just hope I get to see you still."

Tentatively, they both glance at me as if they know it's my decision and not my fiancée's.

"Of course you will see her," I say firmly. "I'll make sure of it, Ida."

The older woman nods gratefully and kisses Monroe's cheek. "I'll see you again soon then, honey."

"See you soon, Gram." Monroe tightly embraces Ida, and we wave her off as we walk back to the car. She doesn't say a word as we get in and start driving back to my place. I let her process everything that's happened without interrupting. Once she has something to say, I'm sure she'll tell me.

And finally, Monroe turns to me as she says, "Thank you for letting me have that. Even if you didn't mean it when you said I could see her again... it meant a lot."

"Of course you'll see her again." I keep my eyes trained on the road. "I know you think I'm a monster, Monroe, but I will give you what you want sometimes."

"Only sometimes?"

I glance at her to see a smile playing on her lips. "Maybe more often if you're a good girl for me."

"How can I be a good girl for you?"

I stop the car on the side of the highway. Several vehicles blow their horns at me, but I ignore it, walking over to her side of the car and pulling Monroe off the passenger seat by her hair. She shrieks but doesn't fight me as I throw her over the hood of my car.

Monroe's eyes are wild as they follow me. I round the hood, watching her, knowing her heart is racing as she waits for what's about to happen. The moment I'm next to her again, I tear her blouse off. She shrieks again, trying to cover up her chest as her panicked eyes watch the passing cars.

"Are you crazy?" she demands, panicking.

"Yes." I nod. "And you fucking love it."

I flatten her back against the hood of the car and spread her legs. I make quick work of getting rid of her panties as horns blare at us from passing cars. But there's no way for someone else to stop here. No one's going to bother us.

By now, Monroe's moaning. I part her legs and bury my mouth between them, sucking and drinking from her dripping pussy like it's a tap.

"Alaric, stop it!" she hisses through gritted teeth.

"Your pussy doesn't want me to stop," I hiss against her wet lips. "Your pussy wants to come."

She groans, but at the next moment, her body twists in pure pleasure as my mouth returns to her center. I suck on her sensitive clit until she's banging her little fists against the hood of the car. She wants this. She's desperate for it. She's not even denying it anymore.

"Come on my tongue," I demand. "I want to feel you letting go in front of all these cars, all the people watching. Fucking give in, Monroe."

"No!" She twists and turns beneath me, but I don't let her get away. And then my tongue hits a spot that's like a switch. Her body stops flailing, and she arches her hips into my mouth. I smirk against her skin, licking at her center until she's whimpering for help that isn't going to come.

"You love it," I grunt. "You love everyone watching us. You loved it with the Lombardis too, didn't you?"

"N-No."

Her telltale stutter is a tell, and she knows it, flushing deeply as I continue licking orgasm after orgasm out of her body. She's crying, whimpering, and mewling like a kitten as I tire her body out. At first, she still twists and turns after each one, but I can tell she's wrung out when she just lies back and moans my name over and over again.

The cacophony of the horns blaring melts into nothing as I pick Monroe up and place her back in the car. I put her seat belt on and cover her with my jacket while I drive us home. She's so far gone she keeps falling asleep on me. I should feel guilty about what I did to her, but I fucking don't. I loved every second of it.

And I know my sugar did, too, even though it will take her a while to admit it.

Once we get home, I carry her to bed and get in beside her, telling myself it's just so I can make sure she's not going to try to run or do something equally stupid.

But as I lie in bed next to Monroe, I find my thoughts circling back to what Ida said.

That I shouldn't marry her unless I love her.

On some level, I agree with her. I always thought if a woman could force me into getting married, she'd have to mean a lot to me. Perhaps even enough for the l-word. So why am I not fighting this marriage with Monroe harder? It was my idea in the first place.

Maybe, deep down, I've already accepted my feelings for Monroe.

But I'll be damned before I admit them out loud.

19

MONROE

*Y*esterday, I felt like my life was a nightmare. Today, it's still a dream but not a bad one anymore. Alaric showed me a new side of him, one I didn't think could possibly exist. He's trying to take care of Grams and me. I'm still having a hard time trusting that he doesn't have ulterior motives, but I can't think of any reason he would have to coerce me into doing anything.

He's proven time and time again that he has the means and the lack of morals to take what he wants. He doesn't have to care, yet he does. He went out of his way to make sure my grams is comfortable and her housing is paid for. That's all I ever wanted.

"Thank you for doing this. Paying for my grandma's place."

"That was the deal, wasn't it? You do what I want. I give you money."

"Yeah, but I feel like it's more than that now. I mean, I hope so at least since you are adamant about marrying me tomorrow."

"Yes, it's more than that now, but I need you to understand that I still have needs. I still crave things you are not going to like."

"I know, but as long as you take care of my grams, I'll let you do whatever you want to me. If you want to drug me again, I'm okay with it. I just... I don't want someone else to touch me."

"You know I would cut someone's hand off for touching you."

The image of Alaric cutting off that man's hand the other night pops into my head. For normal people, that would sound like an idle threat, but I know Alaric is dead serious.

"You let other people watch," I whisper, regretting that I said it at all immediately.

"Watching and touching are two different things… Besides, it was that or you killing someone for the family."

"I could never kill someone."

"I know," Alaric says, just as he pulls into his garage. I was so lost in the conversation I didn't even realize we were here. He cuts off the engine, and we both get out of the car.

"Do you want to do it tonight?" I ask when we are inside the house.

"Maybe I already put something in your tea earlier." Alaric smirks.

"Did you?" A mixture of fear and excitement builds in my lower abdomen.

"No. But I have been thinking about it," he admits. "Actually, I've been thinking about trying something new."

"New? Like what?"

A sinister smile spreads across Alaric's face, and like the predator he is, he stalks around me. I'm a deer caught in the headlights, frozen in place, while Alaric moves behind me to help me out of my jacket. The small hairs on the back of my neck stand up, and my entire body is on high alert, warning me of the imminent danger. Yet I'm still just standing here like an idiot.

Alaric steps closer until his chest is pressing up against my back, and I can feel his hard cock rubbing against my ass. He swipes my hair away from my shoulder, exposing my neck and letting me feel his minty breath on my cheek when he talks.

"You know I like the part when you don't know when it's coming. I love controlling that, controlling when and how... controlling *you*."

I'm still trying to digest what he is saying when I feel it. The sharp prick of a needle entering my neck. I suck in a quick breath as the pain cuts through me, then quickly dissipates. Before I can even think about fighting or running away, my legs give out, and my body is held up by a thick arm around my middle.

"Www..." I start, but my tongue stops working halfway through the word. My whole body simply gives out, and I'm picked up off the ground and carried through the house.

I'm waiting for my mind to go as well, for the darkness to drag me under, but my mind stays awake and alert. *What the hell?* I start to panic, pushing my limbs to move, working my lungs up for a scream, but nothing happens. It's almost like I'm... paralyzed.

"You're fine, Monroe. Don't be scared," Alaric assures me, but right now, his words mean nothing to me. I'm fucking paralyzed. I can feel, I can think, but I can't move. This is not what is supposed to happen. Maybe he gave me the wrong drug. Perhaps he is killing me without knowing, or he changed his mind, and he is killing me.

Alaric carries me to the bedroom, gently puts me down on the bed, and props the pillow under my head so I'm comfortable and can see him. Sitting down next to me, he starts unbuttoning his shirt.

"I gave you a special kind of sedative. It paralyzes your body without making you go to sleep or numbing you up. You'll be awake, and you'll be able to feel. You just won't be able to move or talk," he explains while undressing himself slowly. "It will only last for about an hour."

A tiny bit of panic recedes. At least I know the drug is working the way it's supposed to, and I won't be paralyzed forever.

"I want you to see and feel what I do to you when you're asleep. I thought about taking a video, but that wouldn't be the same. I've used this drug before, so I know this would be perfect."

He's used this drug before? He's done this to someone else? Unwanted jealousy weasels its way up my spine, and I hate that I feel this way at all. What a fucked-up thing to be jealous about.

"I haven't used this drug for sex before if that's what you are thinking," he says as if he was reading my mind. "I've used it to kill someone slowly and painfully. Someone who didn't deserve a quick death."

Alaric stands to step out of his pants and underwear before he turns and undresses me. He touches me like I'm made of glass, gentle and careful. When I'm completely naked as well, he spreads my legs apart and moves between them on the bed.

"Do you see how hard you make me? Fuck, my balls hurt thinking about being inside you. This is what you do to me, Monroe. All I think about all day is being inside your tight cunt. I've never wanted anyone so bad, only you."

He starts stroking his cock, and I'm both terrified and curious about what he will do to me. He reaches for something beside him, but I can't turn my head to see what it is. I hear something being opened, like a bottle cap maybe. A moment later, I realize he is squirting something in his hands, then he rubs it over his dick.

"It's just some lube to make sure I won't hurt you," he explains.

He moves closer until I can feel his thighs touching mine. Letting go of his cock, he reaches between my legs and runs his fingertips through my slit ever so gently. His skilled fingers draw small circles over my clit, igniting sparks of pleasure in my core.

If I could, I would probably moan, arch my back, or lift my hips to meet his hands, but all I can do is lie there and feel it. After a few moments, his fingers slide farther down and slip into my pussy with ease.

He pumps his finger in and out a few times before withdrawing and sliding down farther between my ass cheeks. No. No. No. I want to tighten up, squeeze my butt together, but I can't do anything as he massages my puckered hole.

"I told you this was mine as well, and you said I can do whatever I want." He smirks. "This is going to be perfect because you can't clamp up, and that's what makes it hurt. Being relaxed and unable to move is going to make for a pleasurable experience. You're going to love getting your ass fucked." And then he forces his finger inside my ass.

I expect it to hurt badly, but it's simply a light uncomfortable sting. He starts pumping his finger in and out of my ass with ease, thanks to the lube. It feels so wrong, dirty, depraved... yet I don't want him to stop. My nerve endings inside my ass are on fire, shooting waves of pleasure straight to my core.

Only when he adds a second finger does it get uncomfortable again. Then he adds a third. Oh god. Just when I think I can't take the pressure any longer, he pulls out of my ass and shoves all three fingers into my wet pussy.

I almost come right then and there.

He starts finger fucking me with lazy strokes while his other hand roams over my body with a featherlight touch. Leaning in, he starts kissing my stomach and up my breast until his mouth is on my right nipple, swirling his tongue around it and sucking lightly.

Another wave of pleasure crashes into me, and I know I'm going to come soon. Closing my eyes, I do the only thing I can and give in to the feeling.

I don't know what I expected Alaric to do when I was unconscious, but it wasn't this. When he drugged me before, I just know I woke up sore. I figured he manhandled me and took me roughly. Maybe I was simply sore because it was my first time.

Because right now, he's doing the opposite of manhandling me. He is worshiping my body, touching every inch of it like he wants to memorize every curve of me.

He switches to my other nipple, giving it the same attention while moving his finger in and out of my pussy faster. When he adds pressure to my clit, rubbing it with the rough pad of his thumb, I come undone.

The orgasm slams into me like a tidal wave that almost knocks me out. My mind is reeling, but my body remains still, unable to move an inch. All I can do is let the intense feeling run through me.

"I felt your cunt squeeze my finger. Did you just come, Monroe? Do you like being helpless and unable to tell me no? Do you like me doing whatever I want to you? Because I think you do. I think you like being a little toy, letting me use you however I see fit."

I want to deny him. I want to tell him that he's wrong, but I already know that would be a lie. I don't know if he twisted me to be this way or if I was like this all along, but the result is the same. I do like it. I like what he does to me, no matter how wrong and depraved it is.

"Now that you're all relaxed and loosened up, I'm going to take your last virgin hole. I'm going to make you mine in every way."

If it wasn't for the endorphin rush still swirling around in my brain, I would probably be scared right now.

He lifts my body off the bed and carefully turns me around to lie on my stomach. He moves the pillow from under my head and stuffs it under my stomach instead. He turns my head to the side and swipes the hair out of my face, making sure I'm comfortable and able to breathe well before he moves behind me and between my legs.

The sound of the lube bottle being opened again meets my ear moments before a cold liquid trickles down between my butt cheeks. I can feel Alaric's finger on me a second later, massaging in the lube. At first just around my puckered hole, but then he enters me again, two fingers at a time.

The feeling is still foreign but not as weird as it was the first time. He fucks my ass with his fingers for a few minutes, stretching it until he is sure I can take his cock.

"I think your ass is ready, Monroe. I think my cock is gonna fit nicely in this tight hole. And I think you're going to come harder than you ever have."

He removes his fingers and replaces them with the smooth head of his dick. Slowly, he pushes inside my back entrance. If I could talk, I would tell him to stop or at least slow down. But he just keeps pushing his too-big cock inside my small hole, stretching me so much I think he might be tearing me open.

I feel so full, so much pressure, and for the first time tonight, I'm desperate for him to stop. That thought pops like a balloon on a needle when Alaric snakes his hand around to play with my clit. His fingers draw firm circles over it while he fucks my ass in slow but deep thrusts.

The discomfort rapidly dissipates, leaving behind a pleasurable sensation that soon turns into pure bliss. How can this feel so good?

"Fuck, Monroe," Alric murmurs into my hair before swiping it away to run open-mouth kisses over my neck and shoulder. "You feel so fucking good. You're perfect. Every single inch of you is perfect, and the best part... you're all mine."

My eyes flutter close as another orgasm slams into me. It comes suddenly but seems to go on forever. In my mind, I moan, my back arches, and my muscles tighten, but in reality, I'm completely still while my release runs through my body like a silent storm.

Alaric is still fucking my ass when I come down from my high, but his hands are now holding my hips, keeping me in place as his thrusts become erratic and his grunts turn louder.

"Fuck, I'm going to blow a load deep into your tight ass…" With one last violent thrust, he buries his cock in my ass and holds himself there while coating my insides with his cum. His body goes slack on top of mine, and for a second, I panic. He is so heavy it's hard for me to breathe, and I have no way of letting him know.

Luckily, he shifts his weight and gets off the bed a moment later, letting me breathe easily again. I follow him with my eyes as much as I can, watching him disappear into the bathroom and return with a washcloth in his hand.

He uses the cloth to wipe between my legs. It's warm, and he is being so gentle that it actually feels good against my still sensitive skin. He takes his time cleaning me up, then throws the washrag into the laundry basket.

When he climbs back into the bed, he sits up with his back against the headboard and lifts me off the mattress. I still can't move, but he has no trouble maneuvering my body to pull me onto his lap and cradle me against his chest. I know I should be mad at him, furious for violating me like this, but right now, I simply feel content. My body and mind are worn out, but I feel safe and taken care of.

My limbs are heavy and useless, and my eyelids are starting to feel the same way. I want to stay awake and talk to him about all of this, but I'm so tired. I can talk to him tomorrow. With my cheek pressed against Alaric's firm chest, he strokes my hair, and I let the steady beat of his heart lull me to sleep.

20

ALARIC

Today is the day I'm getting married. The day I officially make Monroe mine, whether she likes it or not. After tonight, there will be no way for her to escape.

I feel a strange sense of unease as I button my vest. Alessandro and Savio are in the room with me. The leader of the Lombardi family drags on a cigar, watching me closely.

Unfortunately for Alessandro, I know exactly what's on his mind —or rather, who.

And he's not getting her, not at any cost and not any price.

I do my best to act polite around Alessandro, but aim most of the things I say at his half brother, Savio. The other man smirks as he begins to notice me snubbing him.

"You seem distant today, Alaric," Alessandro tells me sharply. "I hope this marriage won't affect the work you do for us. Remember, you have a weakness now."

I know he's talking about Monroe. My hands form fists at my sides as Savio claps me on my back, muttering in my ear, "Ignore him."

I give a barely perceptible nod, but Alessandro isn't done yet.

"You know I mean your future wife, don't you? I'm sure you don't want to see her hurt, Alaric. Not on her wedding day."

I pounce forward, but Savio steps between us before my fist makes contact with his brother's jaw. He turns to Alessandro, hissing, "You're drunk. Get out of here, go to one of your whores or something."

Alessandro smirks in response as he stumbles out of the room. I'm still rattled, so I appreciate the tumbler of whiskey Savio forces into my hand.

"Drink. You'll need nerves of steel for the day ahead of us."

I drink in deep, thirsty gulps.

"The party was a mistake," Savio mutters. "We never should've taken it as far as it went. We shouldn't have made you do that with Monroe."

I nod just as Alessandro appears back in the room. I tense up right away. I've seen him like this before, and I know full well the prick is just looking for trouble. But my hands are tied. Alessandro runs the Lombardi family, and by pissing him off, I don't just risk my job. I risk my life and Monroe's, too.

"Why are you telling him that bullshit?" He laughs. "We're like family, aren't we, Alaric?"

"Of course," I lie through gritted teeth. Either Alessandro is too drunk to sense my mocking tone or he just doesn't give a damn as he saunters forward, grinning at me.

"We're brothers, Alaric. My father brought you up just like he did Savio. Like one of us."

I nod, remembering the beginning of my career with the family. They did everything for me. Savio and Alessandro's father was a cruel man, but he showed me an unexpected kindness when he took me in as a sixteen-year-old kid with nowhere to go.

"But women..." Alessandro smiles. "They're nothing but whores. Whores to share and get rid of when they are all used up. Wouldn't you agree, Alaric?"

The smile I force onto my face takes every ounce of self-control I have left. "Of course, Alessandro."

This finally shuts him up, and he saunters out of the room while Savio tries to calm me down with only a few minutes remaining before the ceremony I'm already dreading. Not because of Monroe, fuck no. I'm dreading it because Alessandro will be there, and I just know he's poised to jump at my woman again.

I need to keep Monroe away from him, that's for sure. He's barely holding back today. If I leave it longer than this, he'll jump her bones, and I'm not letting that fucking happen. If I'm forced to choose between my life and saving Monroe from this prick, I'm afraid I'll pick the latter.

Vowing to myself to keep the two separated, I follow Savio out onto the mansion's terrace. There's a makeshift altar set up along with an arch of red roses. It looks pretty, if there was no ominous tension in the air. But the air is thick with anticipation, and my stomach sinks with dread. I have this inescapable feeling tonight won't end well.

There are only about ten men here, all part of the Lombardi family and their employees. My eyes scan the crowd.

Savio and Alessandro are half-brothers and heirs to the Lombardi family after the passing of their father, who started me in their twisted, dark world.

There are three guards whose names I don't know—tall, beefy guys who women fawn over... until they find out who they work for. I think two of them are twins, and the other is Savio's other half brother—not related to the Lombardis but taken in under their wing just like I was.

The other five are men who work for the Lombardis in various positions. I recognize one of them from the night of the party when I was forced to fuck Monroe in front of everyone.

I remember that night as my cock grows heavier. Maybe marrying Monroe isn't such a bad thing, after all. Maybe we can make this work for us. Maybe we won't make each other as miserable as I fear we will.

But the fact remains, Monroe is at my mercy, and I'll use force to get what I want if I have to.

This is the life I chose, and now Monroe is a part of it.

After tonight, she'll be my wife in good and bad, in sickness and in health. And no one will be able to take her away from me ever again.

She's stuck by my side, whether she likes it or not. I want to believe I'm growing on her, that she wants this, wants me, but something tells me she might keep fighting me. I must be one sick fuck, but I'm looking forward to putting her brattiness to rest once and for all.

21

MONROE

*L*ike every woman, I've envisioned my wedding since I was a little girl. Prince Charming sweeps me off my feet and asks me to marry him in a romantic proposal. We get married on a beach or maybe in an old barn with a flower arch. In none of my fantasies did it happen like this.

Alaric is no Prince Charming. I didn't even get a proposal, and this wedding is not the happiest day of my life like it's supposed to be.

The house we're getting married in is beautiful, and even the dress is gorgeous, but everything else is wrong.

"You look very pretty," Ciara tells me. She is about my age but apparently has been working here at the Lombardi residence since she was fifteen. It's a piece of information she dropped earlier, and I'm not sure if it was an accident or not.

"Thank you for helping me get ready." I don't really know her, but I'm so glad I didn't have to do this on my own. I don't know any more people here except the men who made Alaric fuck me in front of them. To say I'm uncomfortable around them is an understatement.

"No problem, it's been nice to get away from my normal duties." She smiles, but it quickly falters. She's been like this all morning. Every time she says something, she seems nervous about it as though she worries she says something wrong.

"How did you end up working here?" I ask as Ciara pins up my hair. Her hands freeze for a second before she continues taming my locks without a word. I don't ask again because I don't want to pry, but I make a mental note to ask Alaric about it later. Something is off about this whole situation, and I'm going to figure out what it is.

The room settles in an uncomfortable silence, which is only broken when someone knocks on the door, making both of us flinch.

One of the guards opens the door and sticks his head into the room. "They are ready for you."

"Can we have another minute?" I ask, hopeful for a little more time.

"No, you are expected now," he snaps, crushing my plan to stall. I guess it doesn't matter if I do this now or in an hour. It's inevitable either way.

"Good luck," Ciara murmurs as I get up from the chair.

"I really wish you could come with me," I tell her.

She immediately shakes her head. "I'm sorry. I don't think I'm allowed to."

Allowed to?

"Enough small talk. Hurry up," the guard urges impatiently. "I don't have all day."

Despite his growing irritation, I give Ciara a quick hug. My arms wrap around her body, and for a moment, she simply stiffens as if she wasn't expecting this kind of affection. Just when I think she won't hug me back, her arms come around my torso briefly, and she squeezes slightly.

I release her, and we share a sad smile before I spin around and follow the guard out into the hallway. I wonder if I'll see her again. I hope I do.

The guard leads me through the house, past multiple armed men standing guard at every exit until we make it out to the backyard. Alaric is standing at the edge of the terrace with a priest beside him. Savio and a few other men are also here. I count five total.

There is no music playing, and all the other people are randomly standing around or sitting on the outside furniture. There are no decorations, no family and friends, no happy memories to be made.

I walk up to where Alaric is standing. Stopping right in front of him, I tilt up my head and gaze at his face. He doesn't like that he is in awe of me or even that he finds me beautiful. His eyes are cold, empty, harsh. It's like he doesn't want to be here, and I don't understand what is happening.

He wasn't like this last night or even this morning. The things he said, the way he made me feel, was it all fake? Or did he simply change his mind? I'm about to ask him if he still wants to do this when he suddenly turns away from me to face the priest.

"Begin," he orders. "Just do the basics. No need to draw this out."

I wince, feeling like I've just been slapped.

"Yes, hurry up, Father, so we can celebrate this union with a party." Alessandro laughs, and my stomach churns. I do not want to be here for another one of his *parties*.

The priest rushes through the whole wedding, cutting it so short, it doesn't take more than five minutes until we are officially married. There is not even a kiss at the end. This must be the least romantic wedding of the century.

"You can go now," Alessandro dismisses the priest, who can't get away fast enough. "Let's eat and drink some champagne." He claps his hands together in excitement and heads inside.

Alaric holds out his arm, and I loop mine around. We follow Alessandro even though all I want to do is run in the opposite direction. The other men follow as well, and I recognize two of them from the other night.

"Can we leave?" I whisper so only Alaric can hear.

"Not yet." He shakes his head without even looking at me. His jaw is set in a tight line, and his eyes are full of anger. Why is he so angry? Does he hate being married to me that much?

Tears prick at my eyes at the realization that this is my life now. I'm married to a man who doesn't love me and who possibly even hates me. A man who kills people for a living and wants me drugged so he can fuck me any way he wants to.

With every step I take, I feel more and more like I'm being led to slaughter. Alaric leads me to the dining room, where the table is already filled with a buffet of food that looks like it can feed an army.

Alessandro pulls out a chair for me, pretending to be a gentleman of sorts, and I have to hold back a snort at his gesture. I force a smile and take the seat. Alaric sits down on my right side, and unfortunately, Alessandro takes the one on my left and the head of the table. Savio sits across from me, and the other two men sit next to him. I don't know either one of their names, but I recognize one of them from the other night. He was holding a camera up, videotaping me. A shudder runs down my spine at the memory I rather want to forget.

Even with Alaric acting as he has been, I want to scoot closer to him, nestle into his side, and bury my face into his chest. No matter the way he treats me, he is still my only protector here, the only one who has shown me kindness.

"I don't know if your new husband has told you, but you look delightful today," Alessandro compliments. "Your tits look great in the dress."

"Thank you," I murmur as he loads my plate with an array of food.

"You better eat up. You'll need your strength for your wedding night." He snickers. "Knowing Alaric, I'm sure he has plenty planned for tonight. I know I do."

Bile rises in my throat at his comment. Does Alaric plan on staying here? Oh my god, he is going to share me with them tonight. The savory smell of the food in front of me turns rotten, and I have to turn my head and concentrate on not throwing up.

"Eat," Alaric adds, making me even more uncomfortable.

With trembling fingers, I grab the fork and start eating tiny bites of the food on my plate. I force myself to eat as much as I can, chewing every morsel thoroughly and taking small sips of water between.

By the time everyone else is done, my plate is still half full, but thankfully, no one says anything, and one of the maids takes my plate away.

"Time for your wedding gift," Alessandro announces after the table is cleared. A moment later, one of the guards sets a neatly wrapped package on the table in front of me.

It looks normal, with white wrapping paper and a silver bow on top, but knowing who bought it makes me wonder if the inside will be as normal. Hesitantly, I unwrap the gift and take the lid off as if I'm expecting a bomb inside.

What I find instead is a silver collar. For a split second, I think he is getting us a dog, and this is merely a clue, but then I remember who he is. The collar is for me.

"That is so you know who owns you. The gift on the bottom is for when you misbehave," he explains. "Go on, look at the bottom of the box."

Grinding my teeth, I take out the collar and the cushion it sits on. Below it, I find something else silver, a butt plug, and it's not small either. It's huge.

"Both come with a remote," Alessandro explains excitedly, "With one push of a button, it sends an electric shock to either her neck or her ass. Trust me, she'll do whatever you want after you do this a few times." He laughs, and the rest of the men at the table join in... including Alaric.

My blood runs cold, and for the first time today, I feel just as uncomfortable having Alaric by my side as Alessandro.

"Shall we try it out?" one of the men at the table suggests.

"She's done well today. I'll keep this one for when she actually misbehaves," Alaric tells them as he picks up the collar to inspect it. "She won't be able to break this?"

"No, once it's on, you can only remove it with the code you set yourself. There is no way she'll get it off."

"Good to know. She hasn't tried to run yet, but I'm sure she will eventually. This will come in handy." Alaric sets the collar back in the box.

Cold sweat runs down my back as fear sets in, real bone-crushing fear. That terror only reaches a new height when Savio chimes into the conversation.

"Alaric, come have a cigar with me at the pool. I'm sure Alessandro will find a way to entertain your new bride."

No, no, no. Instinctively, I grab Alaric's forearm. Digging my nails into his suit-covered arm, I plead with him to stay without saying a word. That hope is crushed when he grabs my wrist and pulls my hand away.

"A cigar sounds great," he says nonchalantly and gets up from his chair. He doesn't even look at me. "Behave yourself, Monroe," he warns before turning around and walking away, leaving me behind more scared and confused than ever.

I watch Savio and Alaric disappear from the room and out to the terrace. The glass door closes behind them, and dread pools in my gut. They walk away until I can't see either one of them anymore, and I feel like someone just died. I'm just not sure who? Did I lose Alaric, or did I lose myself?

All thoughts evade my mind when a hand wraps around the back of my neck. Alessandro's fingers tighten as he forces me to turn back to face him.

"Oh sweet Monroe, we're going to have so much fun together."

My chest heaves, and I feel like I can't get enough air into my lungs. How could Alaric leave me with him? How can he break that fragile trust we had built? I feel utterly betrayed and abandoned. But above all, I'm scared of what's to come.

22

ALARIC

I can hear Monroe's screams echo through the house and move faster. I've heard so many over the years, and not once did it affect me the way Monroe's pained cry does. It feels like a dagger to my chest, cracking open the icy exterior of my frozen heart, creating a deep ache I've never felt before.

Before I met Monroe, I wondered if I had lost my soul altogether and, with it, my ability to feel compassion, to care about another person at all, let alone love someone. But at this very moment, I realize I do love her. I don't even know when it happened; I just know that her pain is my pain. Her life is mine, and I will do anything to keep her safe, even if that means dying.

Without a doubt, I would die for her, which is exactly why I tighten the grip on my raised gun as I speed walk down the hallway. When I get back to the dining room door, I don't pause. I don't wait another minute. I kick her heavy door open and storm into the room like a one-man army.

The element of surprise is the most valuable asset I have, and I use it wisely. Before anyone in the room knows what's happening, I fire the first shot, hitting Vinny right between the eyes. Before his body has time to slumps down to the ground, I've already fired another shot at Bruno. Unfortunately, the bastard twists around quickly, and I only hit his shoulder.

"What the fuck!" he roars while pulling his own gun. But this time, I'm faster. I fire my gun again, hitting him in the side of the head. His body goes slack, joining Vinny's lifeless form on the ground.

"Traitor!" Alessandro spits, drawing my attention to him. He holds Monroe by the neck, a knife pressed against the skin right below her skin. Her face is red, and her eyes are puffy. Tears fall down her beautiful fear-struck face. The top of her wedding dress is ripped, the silky fabric hanging off her shoulder like an old rag.

Rage. All I can feel is unbridled rage flowing through my veins, taking over every fiber of my body. I move on instinct, stepping toward them, toward the woman I love, who needs me more than ever.

"Guards!" Alessandro yells, and I don't miss the hint of fear in his tone.

"They're not coming," I say smoothly. "They are either dead or have turned against you. Not surprisingly, most of them simply hated you and were happy when I offered them an out."

"Take another step closer, and she is dead, you bastard." He digs the knife into her tender skin, drawing both blood and a whimper out of Monroe. I stop, my feet suddenly connected to the floor.

"Let her go, and I will make it quick," I offer. "You might be a vile asshole, but you are not dumb. You know you're not going to make it out alive."

"You are in my house! I don't need to make it out. My men are loyal!" he screams, making Monroe flinch.

"Then where are they now? If they are so loyal, where are they now? Do you think I killed them all in the five minutes I've been gone?"

His face turns red, the vein on his forehead building, ready to explode. He knows I'm right. There is no way I silently killed his twenty guards, plus the other staff around the house. Shots have been fired, and no one is coming for him. He never cared about a single person in his life, and in return, no one cares about him.

"If that's so, I'm taking your fucking slut with me," he sneers. His hand tightens around the knife, and my heart stops. The same heart that was frozen for so long begins and stops beating again, all in the same day.

The blade slices through her delicate skin, and blood runs down her slender throat. I aim my gun at Alessandro's head, but I don't lift it fast enough...

A shot rings out, and I lunge forward at the same time. The knife slips out of Alessandro's fingers and falls to the ground between us. Monroe's fear-stricken face goes ghostly white, her hands clutching at her bleeding throat hysterically.

I drop my gun and reach for her, pulling her into my body. I simply hold her to my chest as I sink to my knee. "Baby, look at me. Let me see," I order, tugging her hand away just enough to see how bad it is.

Blood is trickling down her wound, but it's not deep. He didn't hit an artery. I pull her body close, and she buries her face in my chest and starts sobbing. Her whole body trembles, but I sigh in relief. She is alive—shaken up, but alive.

I take in Alessandro's lifeless body on the floor, a puddle of blood forming around his head. His eyes are open, but they are dull, the life in them already vanished. Savio is standing like a statue behind him with his gun still raised. He came in through the terrace door and shot him in the back of the head. It was his plan. He told me that it needed to be done because Alessandro had lost his way. But even so, Alessandro was still his brother. Evil or not, blood is blood, and Savio just killed his own.

"You did the right thing," I try to assure him, but I don't think he can hear me. His eyes are glued to the man he just murdered.

Another moment passes before the door opens and two guards walk in. They scan the room, quickly assessing the situation. "Boss?" One of them approaches Savio carefully.

"What?" He lifts his head, snapping out of whatever shock he was in.

"The compound is secure. The men who were loyal to your brother are all taken care of."

"We can take care of this too." The second guard motions to the three dead bodies on the floor.

Savio nods. "Yes, take care of this... What about the other staff?"

"The maids and the cook are in the basement like you've asked. None of them were harmed," the guard assures.

"Good work," Savio praises his men, something his brother never did. "You should take your new wife home, my friend." He turns to me. "I'll have one of my men drive you to your place."

"Thank you. I won't forget this, Savio." I owe him more than my life now. I owe him everything. He simply nods and orders his guard to have the car ready for us.

Monroe is still huddled up against my chest, her hands clutching onto my button-up shirt like her life depends on it. I rub my palm against her back and speak softly into the shell of her ear. "It's okay, sugar. You're safe now. Let's go home."

Holding her shaking body tightly, I stand and walk out of the dining room. On my way to the front door, I pass a few more guards eyeing me curiously as I carry my bride outside, but none of them stops me or asks questions. Savio must have been planning this for a while even though he only told me about his plan today.

The car is already waiting for us when I walk through the main entrance. The driver opens the back door for us, and I sit down with Monroe on my lap. The driver closes the door behind us before quickly walking around the car to get back in.

"I thought you were going to leave me," Monroe murmurs into my shirt low enough for only my ears. But not low enough for me to miss the despair in her voice.

"I know… and I'm sorry. It killed me to leave you there, knowing he was going to touch you, but it was the only way to catch him off guard."

"Is he…?"

"Yes, he is dead. You don't have to worry about him anymore. Savio is taking over the family, and he means you no harm."

Monroe lifts her head slightly, her big blue eyes find mine. "He was there too… the other night. I saw him."

The memory of fucking Monroe with an audience rushes back. Yes, Savio was there too, but he was forced into the situation like I was. Neither one of us could have stopped Alessandro that night, not without risking Monroe's life.

"He made sure those videos got deleted, and no one will ever know about it. He gave me his word, and that means a lot in my world."

She doesn't look convinced, but she must be satisfied enough with my answer because she buries her face back into my chest. I keep my arms around her like a secure blanket, sprawling my fingers out to cover half of her back. I can't wait to get this dress off her, to inspect every inch of her body and make sure she isn't hurt. I will tend to every tiny scratch, every bruise and blemish until she is healed and happy.

We spent the rest of the ride in silence, which I don't particularly mind. It gives me time to think and reassess. Besides watching three men I've known for years die today, I discovered that against all odds, I'm still capable of loving a woman, and now I'm married to her. The threat against her life has been eliminated, but I still have to make her love me, to make her want to be married to me.

She clings to me at the moment, but most of that could be conditioning. I've protected her from monsters even crueler than me, but I also kidnapped her. Not to mention that I've used her to play out my sick fantasies. Worst of all, I don't think I can stop.

So the question is, will I ever be able to make her want to stay because she wants to, or will she be my prisoner for the rest of her life? Either way, I'm never letting her go.

By the time the car pulls into my driveway, I'm sure Monroe has fallen asleep, but as the driver parks, Monroe perks up. "I can walk now," she announces.

"All right," I agree. I don't particularly want her to, but at this moment, I think it's more important to let her have a little bit of control for once.

The driver opens the door for us, and Monroe shimmies out of my lap, her plump ass rubbing over my dick in the process. Even with all the shit that's happened today, my cock roars to life, making me groan.

I get out of the car, staying close behind Monroe just in case she has the dumb idea to make a run for it. I unlock the door, and she scurries inside the house, heading straight to the bedroom. Locking the door behind us, I wonder why she's in such a hurry.

As I enter the bedroom, I find her wedding dress in a heap on the floor, and the sound of the shower running meets my ears. I follow her into the bathroom, surprised when I find her already in the shower, her lacy underwear still clinging to her body.

"I feel dirty. I want to wash his touch away," she explains while peeling off her lingerie. I start undressing as I watch Monroe scrub her body with soap.

"He'll never touch you again." It's the only solace I can offer her right now. The only peace both of us get is knowing he will rot in hell for the rest of eternity. "Do you want me to join you in the shower?" I asked when I'm completely naked.

"Since when do you ask permission?"

"Since today. I know a lot has happened today, so you might have forgotten the tidbit about being married now. Marriage in my eyes means we're equals, partners in every way."

"Are you telling me you're going to change who you are, your entire personality in a matter of hours?" She laughs while rinsing the soap off her slick body. My cock is already painfully hard, throbbing with the need to be inside her.

"I never said that. And before you ask, I'm still planning on fucking you however I want to." Maybe not tonight, but soon, I will have her again the way I want to. Tonight, however, I only have one need.

"I think your vision of being equals is skewed."

"You can fuck me however you want in return." I shrug.

"What if I don't want to fuck you at all?" she quips, turning off the shower.

I grab a fluffy white towel from the linen closet. "Then you would be lying, and we don't lie to each other."

She doesn't have an answer to that because we both know I'm right. Monroe steps out of the shower and into the waiting towel. I dry her off, rubbing her whole body gently until every inch of her is dry. Surprisingly, she lets me without a fight, even lifting up her arms and spreading her legs to give me better access. Maybe winning her over is going to be easier than I thought.

"Let's go to bed," I coo, taking her hand and leading her back into the bedroom. We climb into my king-sized bed together, and Monroe reaches for the blanket to cover up, but I stop her.

"Please, Alaric...not tonight. I can't do this tonight."

Ignoring her plea, I move on top of her, blanketing my naked body with hers. "This is for you, not for me. All I want to do is make you feel better. I want you to tell me where he touched you, so I can touch you there. I want to replace every memory with a better one."

Scrunching her nose, she's not convinced. "Tell me where he touched you." It takes her another moment, but then she slowly lifts her hand and points at her upper arm.

I lean down, keeping my weight on my elbows, and pepper soft kisses over the spot. When I'm satisfied with that area, I glance back up at her face. She lifts her hand again, pointing at her chest this time.

Shifting my weight, I cradle one of her breasts like it is the most precious thing in the world. I bring my mouth to the nipple and close my lips around the taut peak. A shudder runs through her body, and I run my tongue over her areola. I give the other side equal attention before I lift my gaze to meet Monroe's.

Her cheeks are flushed, and for the first time today, I see a smile tugging on her lips. She raises her hand and points at her slender neck. I immediately lean down, pressing my cheek to hers as I kiss along her collarbone all the way up to the spot behind her ear. She giggles, and the sound vibrates through me in a way I never felt before.

Her small hands press against my shoulder, and I push myself back up to see where she will point next. Her index finger touches her lips, and a mischievous glint sparkles in her eyes.

"He touched your lips?"

"No." She shakes her head. "I just want you to kiss me."

My lips are on hers in the next instant. I don't remember the last time I kissed someone like this, maybe not ever. Our lips mold together like they were made for each other, like there is no other place for them to be than pressed together in a passionate kiss.

Happiness is not something I'm used to feeling. The warmth spreading through my body is foreign, but nevertheless, I welcome it. I hold on to it, and I'm never going to let it slip through my hands again.

23

MONROE

Days pass by in a blur after the wedding... *wedding*. I still can't believe I'm actually married. Even though I want to forget most of that day, I have to admit that everything that followed hasn't been bad.

There has been a shift in Alaric. He wasn't lying when he said being married means something to him. He wants me to be his equal at least in some ways. He's been giving me more freedom every day. I can decide what to eat, wear, and even where to go. As long as he is with me, he will take me anywhere I want to, which is why I'm surprised when he tells me we can't visit Gram's today.

"Why can't we go?"

"I have something else planned for us today." Alaric winks, handing me the creamer.

"One of your...?" I don't even know what the hell to call it. Kinky sex sessions?

"No." He shakes his head, knowing exactly what I'm talking about. "Not sex, though I wouldn't mind sinking my cock into that tight pussy before breakfast."

"Can I drink this first?" I pour a generous amount of creamer into my coffee and stir it with a spoon. When he nods, I continue. "So what *do* you have planned?"

"It's a surprise, but I promise you're going to like it, love it actually." I'm about to grill him for more details when a knock on the door has us both perking up.

Alaric walks to the door, peeking through the side window before opening it. "Savio," he greets, opening the door wider. Savio walks into the space, and immediately, my stomach is in knots.

Just when I felt a resemblance of normalcy, I'm reminded that my life is anything but normal now. My husband is a hitman who works for the mob. This is my life now.

"What brings you here?" Alaric asks, motioning to the kitchen table. Savio takes a seat but doesn't take off his jacket. *Good, he doesn't plan on staying long.*

"I'm here to deliver the list. I wanted to bring it to you personally." *The list?* Savio pulls a piece of paper from the inside of his jacket and hands it to Alaric, who took the seat beside him.

"Of course," Alaric takes the piece of paper without looking at it. I remain standing at the kitchen counter, holding my cup of coffee with both hands. "I will get that done quickly. I know how important this is… for all of us."

"Do you need me to look after her while you're busy?" Savio asks.

I tighten my grip on the mug. The thought of Savio taking me anywhere alone has me on edge. He never hurt me or has been cruel like his brother, but I don't think he is a particularly kind man either.

Alaric lifts his gaze to where I stand as though he is assessing the situation, wondering if I would make a run for it while he is gone. He hasn't let me out of his sight, and I didn't even have time to think about trying to get away. Now that it is on my mind, I don't think I even want to get away anymore.

I'm well aware that our relationship is not normal. Most people would call it toxic, but the crazy thing is that I've been happier for the past few days than I have been in a very long time. Alaric has been caring for me like I'm his treasure. He tends to every single one of my needs, no matter how small. He gives me his full attention every day and holds me to his body every night.

"I think she'll be all right," he finally answers.

"Good, I'll head out then. Let me know if you need anything else." Savio pushes up from where he is sitting and heads to the door.

"Wait," I blurt out, making him stop mid step. "I just wanted to ask you something... um, about your maid... Ciara."

"What about her?" he questions, his tone almost defensive.

"I just wanted to make sure she is okay. She helped me get ready the day of the wedding, and she was so nice to me." I don't mention the odd things she said or that I'm actually worried about her.

"She is doing fine..." He trails off as though he's thinking about something. "I can bring her by sometime. Maybe for dinner?"

"Really? I mean, yes, please!" I agree eagerly. I haven't had a friend since eighth grade, which is when I started working two jobs to make sure Grams had the money for her medicine.

A grin ghosts over Savio's lips before he turns away from me and opens the door. He leaves, and Alaric locks up after him.

"Get ready, so we can leave. I want to spend the morning with you since I'll be busy the rest of the day," Alaric announces.

I finish the coffee in my hand. Once the mug is empty, I rush into the bedroom to get ready. Alaric is dressed and ready to go ten minutes before I am, but he simply sits on the edge of the bed and patiently waits for me.

"Ready," I call out after I manage to wrangle my hair into a messy bun at the top of my head.

"Great." Alaric smiles, getting up from the bed, and runs his palms down his button-up shirt. The gesture is simple, but something about it is off. It's as if he... is nervous or something. I haven't known him terribly long, but we have been through quite a lot together, and not once have I seen him nervous. That fact is more than unsettling.

"Are you okay?" I ask, a sliver of fear running up my spine.

"Yes, I promise. You have nothing to worry about."

I really hope so.

We leave the house and get into his car. Even with him assuring me multiple times, I can't help but feel uneasy. We drive for about ten minutes, and I spend every second of it searching our surroundings for a clue where we could be going. I still come up empty.

Alaric suddenly turns onto a small road, which leads to a gate of some sort. "I don't think you can drive through here," I tell him when I realize it's one of those upscale gated communities. There is a golf course on the right, and I can see a fancy-looking white building, which I'm assuming is their country club sitting on top of the hill.

"I think we'll be fine," Alaric quips, and I can hear the smile in his voice.

We pull up to the gate, where a man in a dark green uniform smiles widely and waves us through without asking a single question. The large iron gate opens automatically as we drive through.

Okay, that's weird.

I stay quiet while Alaric drives us through the neighborhood. The houses are large, with huge yards surrounding them. Many have pools and small playgrounds behind the houses, and I can't help imagining what it would be like living in a place like this. It's every person's dream, isn't it? White picket fence, a husband, two kids, and a dog.

I'm so lost in my own head that I don't even notice when Alaric pulls into a driveway until we are stopped, and he cuts the engine. Confused, I look around. "Where are we? Who lives here?"

"We do," Alaric explains casually. "I bought it for us."

My mouth falls open in shock. I blink slowly, then gawk at him for what feels like ten minutes, waiting for him to tell me the truth. But all he does is stare back at me with a facial expression I can't read.

"You mean it?" I ask when I finally find my voice again.

"Yes, I bought it for us. I saw it and thought it would be perfect since there is a large guest house in the back that would be perfect for your grams and a live-in caretaker."

I hear his words, but it feels like each one has to trickle into my brain for me to really understand what he is saying.

"I want you to be happy. I don't want you to try to get away from me, even if I want to do fucked-up things to your body. I want to give you everything you want because I want you to give me everything I want in return."

"Okay," I say without having to think about it.

"Okay?" He looks at me like he is not buying it.

"I know we met in the most unconventional way, and yes, you do fucked-up things to me, but you also take care of me, you protect me, and... I love you for that."

"I love you too," he tells me right away, like that huge fact is not new to him like it is to me.

Unbuckling myself, I climb across the center onto his lap. Wrapping my arms around his neck, I pull him into a searing kiss that has my core tighten. He snakes his arms around my torso and pulls me against his body. I moan into his mouth when I feel his cock hardening between us.

"I'm going to fuck you in every single room of this house by the end of the month," Alaric promises.

"I can't wait," I answer breathlessly.

"Careful what you wish for, little girl." Alaric smirks, his pupils dilating. "I've been holding back, Monroe, but I still have urges..."

"I know, and I want you to do it to me... whatever you want. I trust you."

"Good, because I might have put something in your coffee earlier," Alaric admits. This time, instead of fear, excitement fills my veins. I don't know what kind of dark and depraved things he is going to do to me, but I know I'll be safe.

I'll always be safe with him.

24

ALARIC

"Open your mouth, sugar."

Monroe's lips part, her tongue slipping out between them to lick seductively.

"Stick it out. Show me your tongue."

She does as she's told, and I grab her tongue with my fingers, placing a little pink pill on her tongue with a smug smile.

"There you go, sugar."

She swallows thickly, making my cock swell impossibly hard in my pants. Fuck, she turns me on so much. It makes me crazy, how much I want her. I can't stop thinking about her sweet mouth wrapped around my cock. And that's exactly why I gave her the drug I chose for tonight.

It'll enhance my experience, too. From what I've heard, the pill will make my cock even more sensitive, swelling harder and harder until I spill a triple load all over Monroe. I'm a heavy comer anyway, but knowing what this pill will do to me when her lips wrap around my cock makes me even more fucking excited.

"Taste good?"

She nods, smiling shyly. "Sweet, like cotton candy."

I kiss her then, a hard, demanding kiss that steals the breath from her lips. I can't get enough, pulling her tightly against me so I can have more of her. She makes me so damn insatiable, and something tells me I'll never have enough of her.

"Get on your knees," I mutter, pointing at the pillow at my feet. "I want my cock in your mouth, now."

She's eager to drop to her knees at our new house with a heavy thud.

"Unzip my pants."

She makes quick work of pulling my belt out, too, fingers trembling as she slowly pulls my cock out. Her eyes widen at the sight of me, and she licks her lips. Monroe's pupils are already dilating from what I gave her, and when she wraps that hungry little mouth around my cock, I see stars in front of my eyes.

"That's right, sugar." I wrap my hands in her hair and control the way she's sucking me, pulling me deep into her throat. "Take all of it and take it really fucking deep."

She chokes on me, but I don't offer her a reprieve. Instead, I fuck her mouth harder and faster, and when I pull her back by the mane of her hair, saliva dribbles down her chin, and she grins at me widely, already high on the little pink pill.

"Do you love it?" I ask her, and she's eager to nod.

"I love it. I can't live without it. Give me more, Alaric. Give me all of it."

I bury my cock in her throat again, this time to the hilt. I watch her struggle while I grow harder and harder inside her. Then I place my hand on her throat, gently massaging her muscles and forcing myself even deeper, even harder. She lets out a gargled cry, but I ignore it. I know she loves this as much as I do. Her eyes convey just how much she wants me to hurt her.

"Swallow it down," I grunt, and she does, her throat working rhythmically to allow me to go deeper than any man has been before. I touch her throat, feeling my cock inside her through her skin. It makes me fucking throb to see her like this, debased and vulnerable only for me.

When I pull back this time, ropes of saliva dribble down her chin again, this time making a mess of her exposed tits. I smear the clear liquid all over her, getting my hand wet before playfully slapping her. She giggles, and as I walk away from her, she crawls after me.

"Haven't you had enough, sugar?" I ask darkly. "You're just asking for trouble now."

Vehemently, Monroe shakes her head, saying, "No, I need more. I need you to keep fucking me."

I light a cigar and settle in an upholstered leather armchair while she comes to rest between my legs, desperately trying to put my cock back in her mouth.

"Are you feeling the pill taking effect?"

"Y-Yes," she admits.

"Tell me what it's doing to you. Tell me exactly what's happening to your body right now."

"I..." She flushes, those remnants of her shyness still preventing her from speaking. But as I start massaging my thick girth before her eyes, her gaze fills with hunger, and she quickly gets over her timidness. "I feel so horny. I want to rub my pussy on something. All I want is to suck your cock, put it inside my mouth, feel it stretching all my holes out. I want to make you come, Alaric. I want to know I'm the only woman who makes you this hard..."

"Oh, you bet your tight little ass you are." I take a puff of the cigar and toy with her, plunging my cock in her mouth and pulling out in the next second. "You love this, don't you? You never want me to stop."

"Never," she breathes as my cock leaves her mouth with a pop. "Give me more, Alaric! I need more."

"No," I reply firmly. "Why don't you get to work and show me what a useful little toy you can be? I want to sit back and enjoy my cigar. But you are free to do as you please with my cock."

I'm already feeling the tingling sensation of the pill taking effect on my body. It only gets more intense as Monroe puts my instructions to good use. She's sucking, licking, and giving her all to my cock, worshiping it like it's a fucking deity.

"That's right," I mutter lazily, puffing on my cigar. "Be a good girl and prove your worth to me, sugar."

She groans and keeps sucking, and I slowly work on my cigar until I'm certain my first orgasm is coming. Then I set the remains of my smoke aside and grab Monroe by the throat. She whimpers and moans as our eyes connect.

"I'm going to come a lot today," I tell her darkly. "In you. On you. All over you. You understand?"

She nods, rendered speechless. Her eyes are hungry, and she's already glancing at my cock, thirsty for my fucking load. "Yes, I understand. I'll be good for you, I promise."

"Okay, good." I smirk. "Then beg for it like the good girl you are."

"I—" She stumbles over her words, flushing, but then another after-effect of the drug must wash over her. Her face changes in an instant, and now she's hungry for more, no longer worried about embarrassing herself. "Please. You have to fuck me."

"Where do you want it, sugar?"

She gets up and bends down, parting her ass for me. The pure desperation of her behavior makes my cock impossibly hard.

"Right here," she begs. "In my ass, please..."

I groan, wetting my fingers with my spit before carefully placing my thumb on her hole. She shivers as I slowly start working it in, stretching her hole and getting it ready for my cock.

"Is that what you want? You want your tight ass fucked, Monroe?"

"Y-Yes."

"Say it."

"I want my tight... little ass fucked... please!" Her words dissolve into moans as I get up, brushing the engorged head of my cock against her trembling ass. "Put it in, Alaric. I can't wait anymore."

"But I love seeing you suffer like this." I trace my fingertips across the globes of her ass, making her stick it out for more. "You're so pretty when you let go, sugar. Show me just how desperate you can be."

She doesn't give me what I want. Instead, she takes my cock from behind and forces it inside her, wetting it in her pussy first before shoving it in her ass. I grunt her name, unable to hold back. I should punish her for this, but I want her too much, and my hips start thrusting into her before I can stop myself.

"Like that?" I gather her long hair in my fist and make her look back at me. Her eyes are swimming with desire when they meet mine. "Do you like being fucked in there?"

"Yes," she replies, delirious. I feel my first load thickening inside me, ready to paint her from the inside. "Oh my god, yes."

"Get ready for your first present." I tighten my fist around her hair and make her look at me as I unload inside her with a mighty grunt. "Fuck, sugar, you're so fucking tight."

Cum dribbles out of her, forcing my cock out with the amount of it. My still hard dick throbs, covered in my juices, and I watch her sink back to her knees. I don't even tell her to fucking suck it. She's on it before I can fully recover from my orgasm.

"Dirty girl," I mutter. "Straight from your ass into your mouth, sugar. Is that how you like it?"

"Y-Yes," she manages between licks, sucking my balls and my cock into her mouth while her eyes meet mine, sparkling with mischief. "Give me another load, Alaric. In my mouth."

"In your mouth?" I ask softly, rubbing my thumb against her cheek. "So damn eager to swallow. I love it."

She gets to work on my cock again, and this time, she sucks with an unrivaled need. The pill has made her a woman possessed, and she seems determined to suck me dry before the end of the night. My dick is loving it, though. And what I love even more is watching her eat all my fucking seed like the good little slut she is.

I know I'm going to burst again, and it happens without warning. I just spill over in her mouth. She buries my cock inside her, doing her best to take every rope of cum I splatter against her insides. Some leaks out from the sides of her mouth, decorating her in pretty strands of pearl white.

When Monroe pulls back, she's swallowed almost all of it, and the last remains drip out onto the floor. Without asking my permission, she gets on all fours and starts licking it off, even off the black, shiny leather of my shoes.

"Fuck, sugar." I stroke my cock at the sight of her, feeling myself getting closer and closer to another inevitable release. She makes me fucking wild, and I can't bear the thought of not burying my cock inside her in the next minute.

Monroe gives me a bright smile once she's done licking up her second load. I force her up by wrapping my fingers around her throat and walking her to the bed. I let her fall on her back. She doesn't waste any time, spreading her legs open and showing off that pretty pussy just for me.

"You beautiful little thing," I mutter, climbing on top of her. "Are you ready for your last gift from me?"

She nods eagerly, and I straddle her, clasping my hands around her neck as I begin pumping inside her.

"You feel so good," she whispers. "I love you. I love this..."

Her words make my heart tighten, and I lower my mouth against her ear, softly whispering, "I love you too, sugar. But that doesn't mean I'm going to go easy on you. You know that, right?"

"I know," she manages in return, kissing me with no abandon. "I need it. I want it. Give it to me. I want it all."

I start pumping inside her yet again with an unrivaled frenzy. I've never needed another human being this much. Knowing she's fully at my mercy has me harder than I've ever been.

With the moans I get from her, I decide to keep my fingers where they are, massaging her throbbing little clit into an orgasm. Her body twists painfully as she comes for the first time tonight, and I smirk as I feel her pussy tightening around my cock, accepting me deeper, milking me for every drop of cum I have left.

"Take it," I growl. "Every drop, all for you, nobody else."

"All mine," she whispers deliriously as my fingers wrap tightly around her neck. "Fuck, Alaric! Give it to me!"

But I'm not going to waste my load that fast. Not before I'm done with her sexy body and using it to drive me to pleasures I've never felt before.

I bend her in every position imaginable and don't stop until she cries. When the first tears fall down her reddened cheeks, I lean down and whisper in her ear.

"Do you want me to stop?"

She shakes her head, banging her fists against the bedsheets until I fuck her even harder. And now, I finally allow myself the orgasm I've been holding back for so long. With one more powerful thrust of my hips, I unload myself inside her.

I don't stop until my cock is forced out by the amount of cum. It leaks out, staining my bedsheets and making me hungry for her pussy. Monroe deliriously scoops some up and licks it off her fingers, and a dreamy smile settles on her face.

Cradling her in my arms, I slip another pill on her tongue, one to stop the effects of the one I gave her before. I pour some water in her mouth and wait with her until she comes back to me.

"I... I can't... I can't believe we did that," she whispers once her head stops spinning.

"We'll do so much more." I smile darkly. "I have so much in store for you, sugar. If only you knew."

She snuggles against me and holds me tightly. "I can't wait to find out."

EPILOGUE

*A*laric

***One Year** Later*

I always hated the way our wedding went, and I've spent the past year planning to have a redo. I figure our one-year anniversary would be the perfect day, and it was.

We had the ceremony Monroe deserved in the backyard of our home. Her grams walked her down the aisle, while Savior stood beside me as the best man, and Celia stood beside Monroe as the maid of honor.

After hours of dancing, eating cake, laughing, and drinking champagne, we finally tell the last of our guests goodbye. Monroe slides her slender hands in mine and pulls me up the stairs to our bedroom.

"I want you to do it." She doesn't have to explain to me what my doll wants. Her eagerness is music to my ear. *How did I get so fucking lucky?* "Please, I want to do it today," she pleads, and I almost come in my slacks.

"All right." I nod and retrieve the syringe from my dresser. I turn around and find Monroe standing at the end of the bed, slipping out of her white dress. She lets it fall off her shoulders, and it lands in a puddle around her feet.

"You look like a fucking goddess, and I'm about to worship you like one too." I close the distance between us and take the cap off the shot. Monroe tilts her head, and I pierce her skin with the thin needle to inject her with the paralytic.

As soon as the drug is flowing through her veins, I drop the empty syringe to the floor. She sways on her feet, and I wrap my arms around her body to lower her gently to the bed. While I let the medicine take full effect, I strip out of my own clothes.

My cock juts out like an iron rod, ready to fuck my beautiful wife senseless. Monroe's watchful eyes follow my movement as I walk around the bed and pull her body across the mattress until her head hangs off the side.

"Did you know you can take my cock much deeper when you are like this? With your throat relaxed, I can shove my cock all the way in there without much resistance."

I stand at the edge of the bed and cradle her head in my hand, tilting it a little to the side. I position her perfectly. Her lips are parted, but I have to use my fingers to open her mouth wide. I push the tip of my cock into her hot mouth, wanting to go slow. But once the underside of my dick runs over her wet tongue, all resolve is gone.

"Fuck," I roar, forcing my cock into her mouth and all the way down her throat. I fuck her face relentlessly, thrusting deep into her throat, hard and fast. Only giving her small breaks to breathe.

I look at her beautiful face, making sure she doesn't turn blue while tears run down her cheek and saliva dribbles out of her mouth. I want to come down her throat so badly, but I know how good her cunt will feel with the vibrating buttplug I got.

Forcing myself to stop, I pull out of her mouth and take a small break. "Fuck, doll. You feel so good. You have no idea how perfect you are. I'm going to make you come so hard, you won't be able to walk for days."

After I catch my breath, I lift Monroe off the mattress and position her so her feet are on the floor. Making sure she is comfortable and can breathe, I move her head to the side and spread her arms out.

"I got you a surprise, a new toy we are both going to enjoy very much," I tell her as I get the box from the closet. I unwrap it quickly, eager to get this inside her. Grabbing a bottle of lube from the nightstand, I pour a generous amount over the plug and between her ass cheeks.

"I'm going to put this plug up your ass. You're going to take it like a good girl. I know you will."

Slowly, and gently I work the tip of the plug into her ass. The tight ring of muscle doesn't give me much resistance, thanks to the paralytic. Still, I work it in carefully, making sure I don't hurt her. The thick part of the plug finally slips in with ease. When it's fully seated inside her, I press the button at the end, and the vibration starts.

It feels strong on my fingers, so I can only imagine what it feels like to her or what it's going to feel like on my cock. I will know that soon enough.

Lifting one of Monroe's legs, I place it on the bed, spreading her wide open to give me better access. Then I'm inside her. I push the entire length of my cock inside her waiting cunt.

"Fuuuuuck," I groan. Her pussy is so damn tight, the buttplug not only narrowing her channel but also making it vibrate. Fuck me. I'm not going to last long.

"This cunt is going to be the death of me." I pound into her like a wild animal, taken by primal need. Sweat runs down my body while I fuck her without restraint, thrusting into her over and over again until my balls tighten and I feel the tingle at the base of my spine.

I know this orgasm is going to wreck me before it even hits me. My whole body goes stiff as I empty myself deep inside her heat. My release seems to go on forever, ropes and ropes of cum fill her up until I'm completely drained. Drained of cum and energy, I collapse on top of her small body, trying my best to get my erratic breathing under control.

My limbs feel boneless, but I manage to shift my weight off her and lie down on the bed. I use the last of my strength to pull her up the mattress and into my arms. I'm so spent, I almost forget to take the buttplug out of her ass.

Reaching around, I gently pull it out of her backside and set it on the nightstand. "I fucking love you," I murmur into her hair, knowing she would say it back if she could.

I don't know why or how—all I know is that she does, and that makes me the luckiest hitman in the world.

∼

Thank you for reading Hitman, don't forget to check out the rest of this series!

HEAVEN & HELL
WHERE EVEN YOUR KINKIEST DREAMS COME TRUE

Bleeding Heart Press presents Heaven & Hell, a taboo romance series by ten of your favorite best-selling authors.
Welcome to Purgatory, an exclusive club where we transform your darkest desires into reality. Here, everything is possible and nothing is too taboo.
Test your limits and find the kink you never knew you needed.
Newsletter Signup

Books in this Series:
Heaven by Darcy Rose
Hell by J.L. Beck and C. Hallman
Hitman by Isabella Starling and C. Hallman
Poisoned Paradise by Lucy Smoke
Possessive by Vivan Wood
Wrong by Adelaide Forrest
Decent by Sam Mariano
More to come...

Printed in Great Britain
by Amazon